"Bodie!"

Bodie whi_____ as a rifle's shot ra_____ fast along the riverbank as two mounted riders angled to cut off his escape. Longarm leaned forward in his saddle and drew his gun. He had never had much success shooting accurately from a running horse and he didn't want to waste any bullets. But the horsemen were much closer to Bodie than he was and they were about to overtake the kid and shoot him in the back.

Suddenly, Bodie veered hard up the riverbank, disappeared behind a fallen tree, and opened fire. Longarm did the same, and his surprise attack caught the two horsemen off guard. Flanked on both the front and the back, the hired gunmen were caught in deadly cross fire. They tried to make a run for it, but Bodie and Longarm emptied their pistols and knocked them out of their saddles. One man splashed into the river and the other was thrown off his mount and smashed into a dead tree. Their frightened horses stampeded through the cottonwoods and disappeared.

DON'T MISS THESE
ALL-ACTION WESTERN SERIES
FROM THE BERKLEY PUBLISHING GROUP

THE GUNSMITH by J. R. Roberts
Clint Adams was a legend among lawmen, outlaws, and ladies. They called him . . . the Gunsmith.

LONGARM by Tabor Evans
The popular long-running series about Deputy U.S. Marshal Custis Long—his life, his loves, his fight for justice.

SLOCUM by Jake Logan
Today's longest-running action Western. John Slocum rides a deadly trail of hot blood and cold steel.

BUSHWHACKERS by B. J. Lanagan
An action-packed series by the creators of Longarm! The rousing adventures of the most brutal gang of cutthroats ever assembled—Quantrill's Raiders.

DIAMONDBACK by Guy Brewer
Dex Yancey is Diamondback, a Southern gentleman turned con man when his brother cheats him out of the family fortune. Ladies love him. Gamblers hate him. But nobody pulls one over on Dex . . .

WILDGUN by Jack Hanson
The blazing adventures of mountain man Will Barlow— from the creators of Longarm!

TEXAS TRACKER by Tom Calhoun
J.T. Law: the most relentless—and dangerous—manhunter in all Texas. Where sheriffs and posses fail, he's the best man to bring in the most vicious outlaws—for a price.

→●→ **TABOR EVANS** →●←

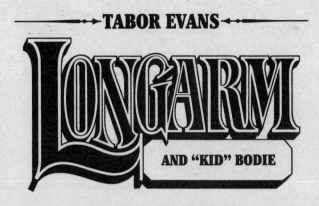

LONGARM

AND "KID" BODIE

JOVE BOOKS, NEW YORK

THE BERKLEY PUBLISHING GROUP
Published by the Penguin Group
Penguin Group (USA) Inc.
375 Hudson Street, New York, New York 10014, USA

USA / Canada / UK / Ireland / Australia / New Zealand / India / South Africa / China

Penguin Books Ltd., Registered Offices: 80 Strand, London WC2R 0RL, England
For more information about the Penguin Group visit penguin.com

LONGARM AND "KID" BODIE

A Jove Book / published by arrangement with the author

Jove Books are published by The Berkley Publishing Group.
JOVE® is a registered trademark of Penguin Group (USA) Inc.
The "J" design is a trademark of Penguin Group (USA) Inc.

For information, address: The Berkley Publishing Group,
a division of Penguin Group (USA) Inc.,
375 Hudson Street, New York, New York 10014.

ISBN: 978-0-515-15307-1

PUBLISHING HISTORY
Jove mass-market edition / April 2013

PRINTED IN THE UNITED STATES OF AMERICA

10 9 8 7 6 5 4 3 2 1

Cover illustration by Milo Sinovcic.

ALWAYS LEARNING   PEARSON

Chapter 1

Deputy United States Marshal Custis Long stepped out of Denver's Federal Building anticipating a pleasant weekend. Denver's early June weather was mild, and he thought he might go to the horse races and place a few bets tomorrow. An even better idea occurred to him . . .

Perhaps he'd invite a young woman that he'd been keeping an eye on and see how that relationship went. Her name was Gloria Harmon, and she owned a popular dress shop just two blocks from his modest, three-story rooming house. They'd been visiting at a café a few days a week during lunchtime, and Longarm enjoyed both her company and her looks. Gloria seemed to be fun-loving and adventurous, and she was always asking him about the places he'd visited and the criminals he'd either arrested or shot. She seemed to take a vicarious pleasure in sharing his adventures, and Longarm had a strong suspicion that she would be a wildcat in bed. Gloria didn't seem to want to tell him much about herself, but that was fine with Longarm. He was sure she was lusty and lonesome, which was always a winning combination.

"Have any special plans for this weekend?" his boss, Billy Vail, asked as he exited the building to stand for a moment beside Longarm.

"Nothing special."

"Well, my wife is cooking a pot roast and one of her prize-winning apple pies tomorrow afternoon, and you're welcome to come by for dinner."

"Thanks, Billy, but I'm probably going to the horse races tomorrow and then out to dinner with a friend."

Billy was not only Longarm's boss, but also his closest friend. They'd worked together for he couldn't even remember how many years and over that time a solid, mutual respect had developed between them. "Suit yourself," Billy said, shrugging with indifference. "If you don't come over to join us, that simply means more apple pie for me."

Longarm chuckled. "Billy, the *last* thing you need is extra servings of apple pie. What do you weigh now, two-thirty?"

"Naw!" Billy tried to look offended. "More like two hundred."

"You haven't weighed two hundred pounds for years!" Longarm exclaimed, poking his boss in the gut and then drawing a cheroot from his coat pocket and lighting it. "I don't mean to be insulting, Billy, but you need to drop a few extra pounds."

"And you need to put a few pounds on," Billy

countered. "That last assignment I sent you on really took a physical toll, Custis. When you came back from Montana, you looked as if you hadn't eaten in weeks."

"I did lose some weight," Longarm admitted. He stood six-foot-three in his stocking feet and normally weighed around two-twenty-five, but a recent hard chase across long, tough miles in the teeth of a bone-chilling wind had been a physical hardship. He'd tracked two outlaw brothers all the way to Helena, and the weather had been freezing, with snow flurries.

"Custis, instead of chasing women you need to rest up this weekend."

"I get bored sitting around, Billy."

"I know that you're a restless spirit." Billy clapped his friend on the shoulder. "But just you remember . . . there might still be a slice of pie left for you on Sunday. And leftover pot roast tastes as good the second night as it does the first."

"I'll try to come by and see you Sunday," Longarm replied, knowing he wouldn't. It wasn't that he didn't enjoy Billy and his wife's easygoing companionship; it was just that he enjoyed his own company after being cooped up in an office all week. And even more than that, he enjoyed the company of lovely women like Gloria Harmon.

"All right," Billy said. "Get some rest, some sleep, and eat well."

"I'll be sure and do that," he replied as Billy headed on down the busy street. Longarm smoked his cheroot a few moments, said good-bye to several of his fellow office workers and marshals, and then headed for a nearby saloon, where he'd enjoy a drink before going to see if Gloria wanted to go out to dinner tonight and maybe—if they continued to hit it off well—to the horse races with him tomorrow.

Longarm was halfway home along Colfax when he stopped and looked up the street, having heard a gunshot and then loud curses. Two big men were beating a smaller, raggedly dressed man while a sandy-haired kid who looked to be about thirteen or fourteen years old was down on his knees cradling the head of a large and badly wounded dog. Suddenly, the smaller man pulled out a derringer and shot one of the bigger men in the chest, killing him instantly. Longarm bolted forward, but before he could intervene, the other large man drew a pistol and shot the smaller man three times. The man dropped his derringer and collapsed.

"No, Pa!" the kid screamed, throwing himself across his father's body.

The big man cursed and then viciously kicked the kid's dead father in the side of his head. The kid grabbed his father's two-shot derringer and screamed, "Damn you!"

Longarm was running hard, but still twenty feet away, when the kid fired the derringer at nearly point-blank range. The big man staggered backward, his face contorted with rage and disbelief. He raised his gun and would have shot the kid if Longarm had not skidded to a halt, whipped out his Colt revolver, and shot the man through the head.

Suddenly, it was over. The boy fell to his knees next to his father's body, and then he crawled over to his wounded dog and cradled its head in his lap.

"Sweet Jesus," Longarm whispered to himself as he knelt beside the boy and his dog. "What a hell of a thing this is."

It had all happened so fast. An initial shot, probably the one that hit the dog, then quick shots and three men were dead. Since Longarm couldn't do a thing for the men, he leaned close to the kid and whispered, "What's your dog's name?"

"Homer," the boy managed to say. "He bit that first man and got shot for it. Then my pa . . ."

"Never mind all that," Longarm said quietly. "What was your father's name?"

"John. John Stock."

"And your name?"

"Bodie."

"Bodie Stock?"

"No," the kid said, "I never knew my *real* pa or last name so I just go by the name of Bodie, which is where I was born and mostly raised. John Stock was my stepfather, I guess, and I liked him well enough."

Longarm frowned, but there wasn't time for a complete explanation, so he carefully removed the empty two-shot derringer from the kid's clenched fist. "I'm sorry that we can't do a thing for your John, but maybe your dog still has a chance. I know a doctor that owes me a favor or two. Do you want to see if we can save Homer?"

Bodie scrubbed the tears from his eyes and cheeks. "He's all I got now, mister. If Homer dies, I'm finished."

"Let me take a look at your dog," Longarm quietly offered. "Maybe he isn't shot that bad."

The boy nodded and rolled over to his father's side. He was still crying, but quietly now. Bodie was big-boned and sunburned, with freckles across his nose. He was a good-looking boy, but thin and ragged like his dead father.

Longarm knelt beside the dog and said, "Easy, Homer. We're just going to see how bad you've been shot."

A low rumble sounded in Homer's throat. He was nearly the size of a winter-starved timber wolf, and Longarm figured that if he'd bitten one of the dead men, he'd bitten the man hard.

"Bodie," Longarm said, after a quick inspection, "I think that your dog might make it if we can get him to a doctor and stop the bleeding before it's too late."

"Mister, I ain't got any money for a doctor. Ain't any money in my step-pa's pockets, either."

"Like I said," Longarm repeated, "I know a doctor nearby who owes me a couple of favors for all the business I tend to bring him in my line of work. So tell Homer that I'm going to pick him up and I don't want him to take a big chunk out of me."

Bodie needed something to distract him from the dead men, so he scooted over to his dog and leaned close to the wounded beast and whispered something. Homer stopped growling, and Longarm slipped his arms under the dog and managed to stand.

"If you want to stay here with John Stock," Longarm said, "do it."

People were already gathering around, and Longarm told someone to get a lawman and a mortician.

"I'm taking Homer to Doc Winslow's office just up the street. I'll be back to talk to you, and we'll take care of John."

"I'm coming with you and my dog Homer," the boy declared, jaw muscles tight with resolve.

Longarm shook his head. "Bodie, you need to stay here with your John Stock. After all, he died trying to protect you."

"Like I said, he was a good man, but he wasn't my real pa or any blood relative, and now he's stone dead," the boy said solemnly. "Ain't any good in me staying here with a dead man. But my dog Homer is alive and I'm going with you."

Longarm stared into the kid's pale blue eyes. They were wet with tears, but there was a fierceness and hardness in those eyes that shouldn't have been present in a boy his young age. "Suit yourself, Bodie."

The dog was huge, but he was all muscle and rib bones and probably didn't weigh more than eighty or ninety pounds. Longarm headed up the street.

"Hey!" someone yelled. "You can't just leave dead people lying by the street!"

Longarm paused and turned to see a well-dressed businessman and a whole lot of people gathered around the bloody scene. "Why not?"

"Because there are *three* bodies, lots of blood, and I saw *you* shoot one of them to *death*."

Longarm raised his voice so that not just this man, but everyone in the gathering crowd could hear him. "Listen, everyone. I'm United States Marshal Custis Long. When a regular policeman arrives—and he will soon—tell him what you saw and that I'll be over at Doc Winslow's office when he needs to talk."

The businessman nodded uncertainly. "I didn't see anything until the kid shot the second man in the chest. I can't believe a kid could do such a terrible thing."

"Well," Longarm said, moving on, "I saw everything, and I'll tell an officer of the law exactly what happened when he catches up with me."

A large and aggressive woman stepped into Longarm's path, and she was pale and shaking with either outrage or shock. "Mister, there's something wrong in the head with a boy who would shoot a man to death and then leave the body of his father lying in the street still warm to the touch." Her mouth twisted and she glared at Bodie. "Boy, I think you're the devil's own child! Yes I do!"

"Get away from him!" Longarm spat. "You've no right to judge that boy! No right at all."

"I seen what he did with my own two good eyes." She turned to the crowd. "And most of you saw the same as me—that boy just put his father's pistol up to a man's chest and blew out his heart!"

Some of the onlookers nodded, also glaring at Bodie.

Longarm was getting angry. "It seems to me that there's a passage in the Holy Bible that says, 'Judge not lest you be judged,' and from what I'm hearing, a whole lot of you folks are gonna be judged, and I hope just as unfairly as you're judging this boy. To tell you the truth, lady, if someone had shot my dog and then gunned down my father and kicked him in the head, I'd have done the same as Bodie!"

The woman started to open her mouth to argue, but Longarm pushed past her and, with the big dog dripping blood all over his coat, hurried up the street to see if the animal could be saved so that the boy had something left to love in his grim and already violent life.

Chapter 2

Longarm barged into the doctor's waiting room that was filled with sick and aged patients. Dr. Winslow's wife, who often assisted him in surgery, glanced up from her desk. Her eyes widened with surprise and then concern when she saw Longarm, the huge and blood-soaked wolf dog, and the pale-faced boy.

"Marshal," she said, coming to her feet. "What . . ."

"This dog has just been shot, and I'd like to see if Doc can save him. He belongs to this boy, and he's all that the kid has left in this world. Do you think . . . ?"

"Of course!"

Nurse Rebecca Winslow hurried forward and said to the curious patients in her waiting room, "We're going to have to see this animal right now. I'm sorry, but he looks to have suffered a bad gunshot wound."

"Go right ahead," an older woman urged, while the others nodded in agreement. "None of us are in danger of dying right away . . . are we?"

The other patients smiled at the grim humor and shook their heads.

"Thank you for being so understanding. Marshal, you and the young man can bring that big fellow into our surgery room."

"His name is Homer."

She glanced back over her shoulder. "Is that the boy's name or the name of his dog?"

"The dog," Bodie said. "He's part wolf and he's a real fine animal."

"I'm sure that he is," Nurse Winslow agreed. "How did he get shot?"

"It's complicated," Longarm said. "Is the Doc tied up or . . ."

"No, he's in the next room examining a patient. I'll go get him. We both love animals, so this is not an inconvenience. Lay poor Homer down on that operating room table and we'll be right back."

When they were alone for a moment, Bodie wrapped his arms around his dog, and there was a quaver in his voice when he asked, "Do you think the doctor can save Homer?"

"I really don't know. Your dog was shot in the chest, but he seems to be breathing all right. Maybe the bullet didn't puncture Homer's lungs but just snapped a rib or something. The doctor will tell us in a minute or two."

Dr. Winslow was a short, energetic man in his early forties who wasn't one to waste time with senseless questions. He burst into the room, took in the scene, and reached for a bottle of something and a patch of gauze. "This your dog?" he asked the boy.

"Yes, he is. His name is Homer."

"How old is the animal?"

"Almost two," Bodie replied.

"Then he's just about your age by our human calendar," the doctor mused. "Is he going to try and bite me when I put this chloroform patch over his nose and put him to sleep for a while?"

Bodie's expression was filled with sudden alarm. "You *gotta* put him to sleep?"

"Yes," the doctor said firmly. "I insist on it."

Bodie reluctantly dipped his head in consent. "Is Homer gonna die?"

"We'll know in a few minutes. Now, hold your dog's head and talk quietly to him while I put him to sleep."

"Is he gonna have to sleep a long time?"

"No. If we can save Homer, he'll regain consciousness in less than an hour."

Longarm stepped back as Bodie cradled his dog's head tightly with both arms. The doc put the chloroform patch over the beast's snout, and Homer jerked back and then relaxed. "Hold the patch over his nose and just let me clip around the wound so I can do a proper examination."

"Aha," the doctor said to himself as he used a pair of surgical scissors to clip away some of Homer's thick brown coat. He gently placed his finger in the bullet hole, wiggled it a little, and then he asked Longarm and Bodie to roll the animal over, which was not an easy job.

"The good news," Dr. Winslow said, snipping away more hair in quick, professional motions, "is that the bullet missed the dog's lung or any vital organs and passed out through the hole on the other side. The bad news is that the dog has lost a tremendous amount of blood and could go into shock and die."

"What can you do for him?" Longarm asked.

"I'll clean the entry and exit wounds, bandage them, and we'll just have to wait and see what happens."

"That's *all* you can do?" the boy asked, looking both disappointed and distressed.

"I'm afraid so." Dr. Winslow found a stethoscope and pressed it against Homer's big chest. He listened intently for a minute and nodded. "Sounds like the beating of a Comanche war drum. Not that I've ever heard a Comanche war drum, but this beast has a strong and steady heartbeat."

"That's good, ain't it?" Bodie asked.

"Yes, very good. We have a little room that we keep supplies in, and that's where we'll let him spend the night. If the big fella makes it until tomorrow, then there's no doubt in my mind that our friend Homer will soon be on the road to recovery."

Bodie sniffled. "I sure hope so. He's a fine dog."

"That he appears to be. At least half wolf, I'd say from the size of him."

"Yep." Bodie raised his chin proudly. "My dog comes from near the Sierra Nevada Mountains same as me. From a mining town named Bodie that's a long way from here."

"Yes, I know."

Dr. Winslow set to work cleaning and bandaging

the wounds, and when he was finished, he said, "I think this dog will pull through . . . but no promises."

Longarm managed a smile. "Thanks, Doc."

"You are welcome. Now, I have an elderly patient that is having breathing problems, and I'd better get back to him right away. Custis, we'll put Homer on a blanket in that storage room, and I'll check in on him now and then to make sure he's all right."

"I'm staying with Homer," Bodie said. "He's my dog and I'm not leaving him."

"I'm afraid you'll have to tonight," Longarm said. "But the doctor and his wife will take good care of him."

"No!"

Longarm looked at the doctor. After a pause, the doctor sighed and said, "Boy, don't you have someone who . . ."

"No," Bodie said, "I'm all on my own now."

"You're too young to be on your own."

"I'm old enough. I can take care of myself, and Homer helps take care of me."

The doctor looked to Longarm for help. "We'll talk this over and get it straightened out," Longarm promised. "I'll take care of it."

"Good," Dr. Winslow said with relief. "We'll move the animal into that room and make him comfortable. He'll wake up in a short time, but he'll be groggy for a while. Now, if you'll both excuse me, I have work yet to do on human patients."

When they were alone, Longarm leaned back against the operating table and said, "Bodie, you can't stay here."

"I have to. When Homer wakes up and finds me gone, he'll be more trouble than any of you can handle."

Longarm realized that this was probably true. "Maybe," he said, "Nurse Winslow can talk her husband into letting you spend the night with Homer."

"If she can't, I'll wait until he can walk and we'll be on our way."

"You can't just leave," Longarm said patiently. "Your stepfather was shot to death and you killed a man. It isn't going to be all that easy."

"Sure it is," Bodie said. "I didn't really know John Stock well. We ain't been together but a few months. The thing is, it would make things a whole lot easier for me and Homer if you can give us a few dollars for eats."

"Who is alive in your family that you can go and stay with?"

"I ain't seen my ma since she ran off with a gambler about two years ago. I got a granny somewhere here in Denver. Her name is Ida, and she's got a house and some money . . . or so I was always told. I don't know if that's true because I never met her. Ida lives with an aunt named Rose."

"Do you even know their last names?"

Bodie cocked his head for a moment in thought. "Granny Ida Clark. Auntie Rose Atkinson. Yeah, that's what John said their last names were. We were going to go find them and see if we could get some money, when those men kicked my dog and shot John and then I shot that last big son of a bitch."

"You shouldn't cuss," Longarm said sternly.

Bodie folded his arms across his chest. "I been cussin' since I was in diapers."

"Well, don't cuss around me or the doctor and his wife, or it won't go well for you and Homer."

"You'd send us off just for cussin'?" Bodie asked.

"Maybe." Longarm was beginning to wish that he'd never become involved. This kid was tough and hard and he didn't seem very cooperative. The other thing was that he seemed a whole lot more concerned about the fate of his dog than about the death of John Stock.

"The room is ready for Homer," Nurse Winslow said, pushing into the surgery. "If we can move him now, it will be better than when he wakes up. I've got a couple of blankets on the floor and he'll be comfortable. I've put a bowl of water and some meat scraps that I sent for so that he can eat if he feels up to it."

"Homer will feel up to it all right," Bodie promised. "He'll eat most anything he can swallow."

Longarm scooped up the dog and soon had him resting on a nice blanket in a small room lined with shelves and a single window. "Mrs. Winslow, Bodie wants to stay with his dog tonight."

"I . . . I'm not sure that's a good idea."

"Then we'll both be on our way when Homer wakes up," Bodie vowed. "We'll get along."

"That doesn't sound at all like a good idea," the nurse said, glancing at Longarm for help.

Longarm fidgeted. He had a problem here and no solutions. He lived on the second floor of a rooming house, and he wasn't about to try to carry that big, half-dead dog up the stairs with a boy in tow.

"Where is the kid!" a loud voice said outside the room.

Longarm turned to see Sheriff Clyde Miller fill the doorway. He and Miller had never liked each other, and Longarm suspected the lawman's recent bad mood was because he was about to lose an upcoming election, which would put him out of a job.

"Hold up there, Sheriff," Longarm said, blocking the big man's path.

"Is that the kid that shot a man down in the street!"

"Sure, but only because the man had just shot his father and then kicked him in the head."

"I'll have to take him into custody," Miller said. "And he's got some questions to answer."

"Bodie needs a little time," Longarm argued. "I'll bring him by tomorrow to tell you his story."

"No," Miller snapped. "Three dead men are lying out in my street, and there's a crowd of more than a hundred. I need to get to the bottom of this now."

Longarm scowled. "Sheriff, I saw everything and I killed one of the men."

"Yeah, so I've heard. And I'll need some answers from you too, Marshal."

"Tomorrow," Longarm growled.

Sheriff Miller snorted in anger. "Well, I guess I could wait that long. But you'd better both come by my office right after breakfast or I'll come and drag that boy by his ears."

"I don't think that's gonna happen," Longarm said.

"You heard what I said. If the kid don't show up at my office right after breakfast, I'll hold you responsible."

Longarm had to bite his tongue to keep quiet. When the sheriff was gone, he said, "Bodie, I'll leave you here with your dog. I'm sure that Dr. Winslow and his wife will bring you and Homer some food. I'll be back around for you in the morning."

"Sure," Bodie said, kneeling beside the dog and stroking its fur. "See you then."

Longarm removed his bloodstained coat and threw it in a corner. Then he left the pair and headed out of the doctor's office, but not before thanking the doctor and his wife.

"The boy looks pretty rough," Rebecca Winslow offered. "Both he and the dog are awfully thin and dirty."

"They've already seen too much of the wrong side of life, Rebecca."

"What's going to happen to the boy?"

"I'm not sure. He says that he has a wealthy granny named Ida Clark and an auntie named Rose Atkinson."

"Ida is one of our patients."

"She is?"

"Yes, she's a lovely old lady."

"Do you know where I can find her?"

"She lives on Center Street. She talks about her rose garden all the time, and the last time she was in she told me that she'd had her house painted a lovely yellow and trimmed with white."

"Center Street isn't that long. I'll be able to find her."

"I hope that the boy was telling you the truth."

"Is a Rose Atkinson a patient of yours?"

"No," Rebecca said. "But Ida has talked about her. I guess she and Rose have lived together for a number of years. I think that Ida said that Rose was a child-less widow and that her husband had died of a fever while searching for gold up around Cripple Creek."

"I'll find them and see if they even know Bodie exists," Longarm said. "Maybe they're able and will-ing to take Bodie and his dog under their roof and raise him up right."

"What about his real mother?"

Longarm shrugged. "Bodie just told me that she ran off with a gambler a couple of years ago."

"And left him?"

"Yeah," Longarm said. "I haven't heard any of the details, but that's what I know so far."

"I heard Sheriff Miller say that the boy actually shot and killed a man."

"He did."

Nurse Rebecca Winslow shook her head. "That boy sure has seen a lot of bad things for being so young."

"He has at that," Longarm agreed as he tipped his hat and went out the door.

He had walked only a short distance when he saw a hearse and two morticians dressed all in black load-ing bodies into their wagon. Longarm was in a hurry and did not want to be questioned about who was supposed to pay the funeral expenses, so he tugged his flat-brimmed hat low over his face and kept mov-ing. No one recognized him, and he continued down the street and then rounded a block and entered the dress shop where Gloria Harmon was waiting on a lady. When she was finished, he approached her and said, "I'm going out to dinner and it would be nice to have the pleasure of your company."

Gloria's dark eyes widened with concern. "Custis, you have blood on your shirt!"

He looked down and saw that it was indeed badly stained. "Sorry."

"What happened to your coat?"

"It's a sad story," Longarm replied. "I need a couple of drinks before telling it. Can you close up a little early this afternoon?"

"Of course."

"I'll just wait outside for you."

"I won't be but a few minutes." Gloria took his hands and squeezed them tightly. "There was a terrible shooting this afternoon just a few blocks away. Is that why you have bloodstains on your shirt?"

"Yeah."

She kissed his cheek. "You need to clean up and get a fresh shirt on before we go out for dinner."

"You're right."

"I have a shirt that will fit, and I think you might like it better if I cooked us something to eat at my place."

"You have any whiskey at home?"

"Only brandy and wine, I'm afraid."

"While you're closing up, I'll get us some whiskey," he said, wheeling around and leaving the shop.

Longarm had killed a lot of men in war and in the line of duty, but he'd never really gotten used to it. And there was something about the ragged boy and his dog that had touched him with sadness. Bodie and Homer were in trouble even before the shoot-out, and Longarm felt that he had to do something to help them or he'd never really forgive himself.

He just wasn't sure how or what he was going to do next, and there was that damned Sheriff Miller to contend with first thing tomorrow morning. But between then and now was Gloria and tonight, and he was hoping that might be enough to take his mind off all his troubles.

Chapter 3

Longarm bought a pint of excellent whiskey and met Gloria as she was closing up her shop. She took his hand and said, "I live just a short ways up the street. Did you get a bottle of good whiskey?"

"The best."

"You sound like you need a few good stiff drinks and someone to talk to."

He nodded. "I had to kill a man just a while ago."

For a moment, her face reflected shock, but then she said, "I'm sure that you had no choice."

"I didn't."

They walked along in silence until they reached the house she rented rooms in. Once inside, Gloria unlocked her door and Longarm followed her inside. The place was much larger than his own, had nice furniture, and was clean. It was obvious at a glance that Gloria took a lot of pride in her surroundings. "Nice place."

"Thank you. I've only lived here six months, so it's not yet the way I like it, but it's coming along."

"Looks plenty fine to me."

Gloria opened the whiskey, poured two glasses, and they sat down next to each other on a comfortable couch. She kicked off her shoes and stretched out, putting her feet on a table. She raised her glass in a silent toast, which he returned. "Make yourself comfortable, Custis."

Longarm removed his boots, slumped down in the softness of the couch, and took a long swallow. He closed his eyes and felt the heat of the whiskey run right down into his belly. Old Oak Barrel was expensive Kentucky whiskey and well worth the price.

"So," she said, "do you want to tell me exactly what happened in that shoot-out?"

"Only if you're curious."

"I am."

Longarm described the unfolding of the events and ended the account by saying, "That kid from Bodie isn't quite normal. He seems as hard as some of the men I've known in war but at a very young age. I'm sure that's because Bodie is used to nothing but betrayal and deprivation given his very grim childhood circumstances."

"And what about his parents?" Gloria asked.

"Bodie says that his mother ran off with a gambler a few years ago. The stepfather that was shot dead today brought Bodie to Denver, probably to dump him off at his grandmother's. The way John Stock was dressed and looked, it was clear that the man was penniless, and it's my guess that he was going

to try to squeeze some money out of Bodie's grandmother, Ida Clark, and also Aunt Rose. Afterward, I
expect John Stock was planning to disappear."

"So you're saying the stepfather didn't really care
much about the boy?"

"I don't think so. And from the way that Bodie is
taking this, the feeling was mutual."

"So what happens to Bodie and Homer?"

"They're staying the night at Dr. Winslow's office.
Tomorrow, I've been ordered to deliver the boy to
Sheriff Miller's office. Miller isn't on my favorites
list. He's tough, ambitious, corrupt, and a bully."

"Yes," Gloria said. "I've never heard a good word
spoken about the man."

"I think Sheriff Miller is looking for something
dramatic to help him win reelection. Three men died
today, and I'm sure he's going to call in the press and
try to make himself look good and in control."

"What do you think will happen to Bodie?"

"I'm afraid that Sheriff Miller might want to tem-
porarily put him in jail and then find some judge who
will force Bodie into a place he doesn't deserve to be
held."

"That would be terrible!" Gloria thought a moment. "But wouldn't his grandmother Ida be his closest known relative and have something to say about
that?"

"I'd hope so," Longarm replied. "But I don't know.
I don't get the feeling that Bodie has ever even seen
his grandmother or aunt, and he certainly hasn't
established any kind of relationship."

Gloria tossed down her drink. "Before you take

the boy to see the sheriff, don't you think we should go find Ida Clark and see if she will help and protect Bodie?"

"That might be the best thing to do," Longarm conceded.

"Well," Gloria said, "before we do that, you need to get a fresh shirt and coat. We don't want you to shock Ida and Rose or make a bad first impression."

Longarm had to admit that she was right. "You have a shirt and coat you say might fit me?"

"As a matter of fact I do. It belonged to my late husband, who was as tall as you." Gloria put her empty glass down and stood up. "Take off your shirt and I'll go get one from the closet."

Longarm finished his drink and poured another. "You sure are all business."

"A boy's entire future is at stake, Custis. My motto is business before pleasure."

"Humph!" Longarm snorted. "Not sure if I agree. And after we find and see if the grandma and the aunt are interested in helping Bodie, when do we get around to the pleasure?"

"In good time," she said, helping him out of the bloodstained shirt. "All in good time."

Longarm had cleaned himself up, and he supposed he should have gone back to his own place for a clean shirt and coat, but he was in a hurry to settle this matter. Besides, Gloria's late husband had had good taste in clothing.

"This must be their house," Gloria said, stopping before a large, yellow two-story building with a beautiful rose garden and a white picket fence. The impressive and well-cared-for home was in one of Denver's most prestigious neighborhoods, lined with tall elms.

"Grandma Ida must have gotten some money somewhere," Longarm said.

"Yes, talk is she was married to a Chicago banker who contracted consumption and came here for the drier climate. He died and Ida sent for Rose, and they've been living here together for quite a few years."

"All right," Longarm said, "let's see what they have to say about Bodie."

When they knocked on the door, an attractive woman in her late forties, with red hair and still a hint of freckles appeared at the door. "Can I help you?"

Longarm removed his hat and introduced himself and Gloria.

"We have something we need to discuss with you and Mrs. Clark," Longarm said, believing as he did in coming right to the point. "Is Mrs. Clark home?"

"Is something wrong?"

"Well, yes and no," Longarm replied. "But I'd rather wait and explain it to you both."

"Oh, dear! This sounds quite serious. Step inside. I'll go get Ida. She's resting upstairs, but I'm sure she'll want to hear what brings you both to our home. Come on in."

The interior of the big house was lavishly furnished with expensive oil paintings, a winding marble staircase, and then a library filled with books. "Please make yourselves comfortable. I'll be right back with Ida."

Rose excused herself and returned a few minutes later leading a tall, slender and stately elderly woman by the arm. Ida's long hair was braided silver, her face practically unlined. Longarm had the feeling that Ida Clark had lived a very good and refined life.

"And so, Marshal Long," Ida said, after more introductions and when they were all seated, "why don't you tell us what brings you and Miss Harmon to our door at this rather late hour of the day."

Once again, Longarm explained what had happened and why a boy and his dog were now in trouble, with nowhere to turn for help.

Ida and Rose exchanged solemn glances several times during Longarm's account, and when he was finished, Ida said, "So you have found and defended my grandson."

"Then you know the boy?" Gloria asked, unable to keep the excitement out of her voice.

"No, I do not. But his mother is my daughter, and if the boy has her wild streak, then he's not going to amount to anything and will probably wind up in prison or on a gallows."

Even Longarm was taken aback. "Mrs. Clark, Bodie is only . . ."

"Marshal, I *know* how old the boy is," she snapped. "When my daughter was with child, I began sending Ruby money. I sent quite a lot of money to mining and boom towns all over Nevada and California. I sent a large sum of money when Bodie was born and begged my daughter to bring him to Chicago to live with me and my late husband. But Ruby always did have a stubborn and rebellious streak. I don't know what I ever did to deserve such a wild child who would, over the span of many years, break my heart over and over again."

"Was she your only child?" Longarm asked.

"No, I had a son. Sweet Elmer died when he was eight, of diphtheria."

"I'm so very sorry."

Rose Atkinson patted Ida's soft and blue-veined hand. "Marshal Long, as you can see and I'm sure understand, Ida and I have both suffered a great deal from the pain caused by the boy's mother. And while we hope that Bodie will turn out to be a good person, we very much have our doubts. Blood, you see, always wins out in the end."

"That's not true!" Gloria said, looking shocked and upset. "This boy has *nothing*. He doesn't know where his mother is or even if she is alive. Bodie told Custis that he never knew his real father, and I'm sure that he never will. Mrs. Clark, you and Rose are the only family this boy has on earth. Surely you can show some compassion."

Ida's face crumpled and tears began to roll down her shrunken cheeks. Her hands fluttered to her chest. "I have a very bad heart, Mrs. Harmon. The doctor says that I am never to get myself upset or my heart might stop. I contribute to many charities here in Denver as does dear Rose. We are good and caring people. It's just that I cannot take any more heartache and disappointment from Ruby or her child."

"But," Longarm vigorously protested, "Bodie has never caused you any heartache."

Ida stood up suddenly, her face tight with strain.

"You just told us that this child named Bodie shot a man to death! Do you not think that in and of itself isn't a heartache to his grandmother?"

Longarm conceded the point with a solemn nod of his head. He came to his feet and turned to Gloria. "It appears that we have come here out of the mistaken belief that Bodie's grandmother and aunt would want to help a boy who has nothing but a badly wounded wolf dog. We had better start thinking of what we need to tell Sheriff Miller tomorrow morning in his office that will help Bodie."

Rose spoke up. "What does Sheriff Miller have to do with anything?"

"He's looking for publicity. He needs some issue to help himself get reelected. I think he'll probably try his best to put both Bodie and me in a very bad light."

"But you are a United States federal marshal," Rose argued. "Sheriff Miller can't hurt you for firing on and killing a man in self-defense."

"That's true," Longarm admitted. "So he'll have to try to smear the boy. Put him in jail or send him to some reformatory or house for criminally insane children."

Rose's hand flew to her mouth and she looked as if she might faint. Ida paled, let out a small gasp, and collapsed deeper into her sofa chair.

"Mrs. Clark," Longarm said, suddenly filled with concern. "Are you going to be all right?"

"Yes," she whispered, "but please go away!"

Longarm straightened and turned away from the two women. "Gloria, we need to go right now."

Gloria looked at the two wealthy and very distressed women and nodded. Nothing more was said as she and Longarm walked stiffly down the polished floor and let themselves out. It was dark outside. The perfume of roses filled the air and crickets were chirping madly.

Gloria linked Custis to her with her arm, and they walked several blocks before either one could think of a word to say. Finally, Longarm stopped under a lamp on a street corner and turned to Gloria. "That went pretty bad, didn't it?"

"It was awful," Gloria replied. "One part of me understands completely why Ida Clark turned such a cold face on her grandson. But another part of me simply cannot understand."

"It doesn't matter if we understand what Ida and Rose feel," Longarm said quietly. "We stated the case for Bodie and they made their decision. Now the boy's fate is in my hands."

"*Our* hands," Gloria corrected.

"But you haven't even met Bodie."

"Doesn't matter. He's a boy, and all he has is that badly wounded dog. If Sheriff Miller plans to use Bodie for his personal and ambitious gains, then I'll fight him, and I can be a pretty formidable opponent when I know that I'm right."

For the first time in a while, Longarm smiled. "Gloria," he said, "I think you and I are going to make a damned good pair."

She looked up, and in the lamplight her face was shining with tears. "You really think so?"

"I'm sure of it."

"I hope so, Custis. Now, why don't we go back to my rooms, pour some more of that whiskey, and I'll make us both something delicious to eat while we figure out what we can do tomorrow morning to protect Bodie from the sheriff."

"I was hoping we might do something to help us tonight."

She laughed. "I think I can guess what you have in mind."

"That right?"

"Yeah."

"And?"

"Let's just have a few drinks, talk, and see where it all leads."

"Hopefully to your bedroom."

"Maybe so," she said, managing a smile. "You're due for something good to happen, I'd say."

"I say so too," he agreed as they crossed the street and walked on.

Twenty minutes later they were climbing into Gloria's large feather bed and then Longarm was kissing and touching all the right places. He found Gloria's pleasure spot, and when she began to squirm and moan, he mounted her and they made love with a passion that surprised them both. When it was over, Longarm rolled off the woman and stared up at her bedroom ceiling.

"How long has it been since you've had a man?" he asked quietly.

"Two years."

"Since your husband."

"No, I had a lover a year after my husband died. We made love at least once a day for two months."

"And then?"

"And then he decided that he didn't want Denver and he didn't want me."

"I'm sorry."

"Don't be. He wasn't that much of a man. I'm better off without him."

"Good."

Gloria rolled over onto Longarm. "So what do we do about Bodie tomorrow morning now that his grandmother and aunt have made it more than clear they want nothing to do with the boy . . . much less his wolf dog?"

"I'm going to sleep on it," Longarm told her.

Gloria reached down and grabbed his flaccid manhood and began to stroke it. "Not all night, you aren't!"

Longarm grinned broadly. He had suspected that Gloria was going to be something special, and now he was sure of it.

Chapter 4

Longarm overslept, and when he awoke, Gloria had already left to open her dress shop. On the kitchen table was a written note that read:

> *Dear Custis,*
>
> *I just didn't have the heart to wake you after such a wonderful but long and exciting night together. As soon as possible, let me know how it went with Bodie and Sheriff Miller.*
>
> *Love, Gloria.*

"Damn!" Longarm whispered to himself when he consulted his railroad pocket watch and saw that it was nearly ten o'clock.

He dressed hurriedly and locked Gloria's door on his way out. His own room was only three blocks away, and he rushed over there to wash up a little, then shave and don his own shirt and coat. He knew that by the time he got to Sheriff Miller's office with Bodie, it was going to be pushing noon.

At eleven o'clock he burst into Dr. Winslow's office to come unexpectedly face-to-face with Ida and Rose. Ida lit into Longarm before he could even ask the old lady why she was here at the doctor's office.

"He's gone!" Ida cried. "My grandson and his dog have disappeared."

Longarm glanced at Rose, who nodded her head and fought back tears. He was about to say something when Dr. Winslow and his wife stepped into the room. The doctor looked upset. "That boy took his dog and left sometime in the night. We had yesterday's receipts in a drawer and that money is also missing."

"How much?" Longarm asked.

"About thirty dollars."

"Doc, I'm real sorry about that, and I promise I'll make it up to you on my next payday," Longarm said. "I don't suppose that Bodie left us a clue as to where he has gone."

"No," the doctor said. "And frankly, I really don't care. I treated his dog for free, we fed the two of them, and this is what I get in return?"

"Again, I'm sorry about the thirty dollars," Longarm said, meaning it. "And I will pay back what Bodie stole."

"Never you mind about that," Ida said. "I'll take care of it. The boy is my grandson and last evening I told you he carried my daughter's bad blood . . . but even so, I feel terrible about judging him so harshly."

"Me too," Rose added. "Neither Ida nor I slept a wink last night, and we were so filled with remorse over what we said about the boy that we rushed over here to the office at first light. Of course, it was locked and we didn't know where the doctor or his wife lived and . . ."

"Never mind about that," the doctor interrupted, cutting Rose off and turning to face Longarm. "The important thing to focus on right now is that the boy is somewhere out in the streets with a dog that is huge but quite weak from blood loss. We're really hoping that you can find Bodie."

"So you can all tell him what a terrible kid he is and that he's not only a killer but a thief?" Longarm asked.

"That's not fair," Nurse Winslow said. "We bent over backward to help the boy after the shooting."

"You're right," Longarm conceded. "It was unfair to say that. But I sure wish that Bodie hadn't decided to run. Sheriff Miller is probably already furious that I haven't brought him by to make a statement. And now we don't even know where to find the kid and his dog."

"We'll help you find him," Ida offered. "Rose and I can join the search."

"Yes," Rose said, her spirits lifting. "We need to find and help him. Maybe there's still hope for Bodie. Maybe he isn't past redemption. Has the boy received any education? Can he read or write?"

Longarm didn't see what that had to do with anything at the moment. "Probably not, Rose." He passed a hand wearily across his face. "I guess we should just start walking the streets. Bodie thinks a great deal of his dog, and he might have gone into a butcher shop and bought Homer meat with part of the doctor's thirty dollars."

"That's a good guess," Ida said. "And we should also visit the cafés and restaurants. You said that my grandson was quite thin. I'll bet that the first thing he did early this morning was to get himself and that dog food."

"All right," Longarm said, deciding that the time for talking about Bodie was over. "I have to go by the sheriff's office and admit that we let Bodie out of our sight and he's disappeared. The sheriff will, of course, be mad as a wet hen, and he'll most likely assign a few of his deputies to also start looking for the boy and his dog. With any luck at all, one of us will spot Bodie and Homer."

"What do we do if he won't come with us?" Ida asked anxiously.

"Try to entice him with the promise of more money or food . . . or whatever you think will work," Longarm advised. "And we'll all meet up at your house."

Ida's eyes widened. "*My* house?"

"Yes. Inside or on that big front porch of yours. If we take Bodie to Sheriff Miller's office, he'll probably be placed under the man's custody, which is the last thing I want or Bodie needs."

Ida and Rose nodded in agreement. Nurse Winslow touched Longarm's sleeve. "I'm sorry that my husband and I can't join in the search, but we have patients to see. I just wish I'd have slept here last night and prevented the boy and his dog from running away."

"I'm not sure that you could have stopped Bodie," Longarm told her. "The boy is very determined, and it's clear to me that Bodie hates being told what he can or cannot do."

"Even so," Nurse Winslow said, "I might have been able to reason with him."

"No sense in talking about it," Longarm told her. "Let's get moving."

Longarm hated to do it, but there was no choice but to go tell Sheriff Miller that Bodie was missing and probably wandering around lost in Denver.

"What!" the sheriff bellowed a short time later. "What do you mean the kid is missing?"

"He ran off with his dog."

Sheriff Miller rose from his office chair and pushed up face-to-face with Longarm. "You promised to bring the boy to me first thing after breakfast this morning. I've been here waiting since ten. Not only didn't you arrive on time, you couldn't even control the boy, and now I've got to spend my department's time and money hunting for the kid and his damned wolf dog."

"Don't bother," Longarm snapped as he headed for the door. "I'll find him and bring him by later."

"Yeah, just like you promised to bring him by this morning!"

"Go to hell," Longarm hissed.

"I'm going to see if I can get your damned badge taken away from you!" Sheriff Miller roared. "I'm going to the Federal Building right now and demand to your boss that you be suspended without pay and then fired!"

Longarm whirled around in the doorway. "If that happens, then we'll *both* be looking for jobs, because as sure as the sun will rise tomorrow, you're going to lose your reelection, Sheriff. You're a disgrace to our profession."

Sheriff Miller howled something, but Longarm didn't hear it over the slam of the door.

Bodie and Homer were lost and very tired. It had grown late in the afternoon, and the sky was dark with the threat of a storm. Bodie had wandered for hours through the city and then found himself in the neighborhoods, some of which were seedy and unsafe. Hard-looking men stared at him, but with Homer at his side, no one approached Bodie or made any attempt to approach him, out of fear of the huge dog.

It would be dark and storming soon, and Bodie knew that he needed to find a safe and dry place to spend the night with Homer. But where? There were so many people here that he felt almost overwhelmed by all the hustle and bustle. His mother had once told him that big cities were bad places to be and that they harbored the worst of mankind. Ruby had warned him to avoid them when he grew to be a man and to find small towns, where people were nicer. Bodie had never quite understood how his mother knew anything about big cities. In all the days of his childhood they had lived in a succession of small towns. And after their experiences there, he considered it to be impossible for people to be any more money-grasping or deceiving than those he'd known over the years.

"We need a place to hole up and hide while I figure this out," Bodie told the dog. "And you need to rest and get strong again."

Homer managed to wag his tail, and Bodie sat down on a low fence and thought hard about what he needed to do to protect himself and his faithful companion and only real friend.

"I've got it," he said at last. "We'll go find a big livery barn and sneak into it to be with the horses. We'll sleep on the hay or straw, and maybe I can even get hired cleaning stalls or currying horses. Give us some time to get you feeling better and me to save us a little more money so we can go back to western Nevada. Maybe even back to Bodie."

Bodie had already decided that he needed to return to the only town that he'd ever really gotten to stay long enough to know. His mother might even have returned to Bodie, or if not there, maybe gone to Virginia City up in the north, which was a place Ruby had taken Bodie many times in her wanderings and search for some permanency in their difficult life.

So Bodie turned, stood, stretched, and headed up the street leading into the heart of Denver. He'd passed quite a few livery stables, and he was just sure that at least one of them would give him and his dog a place to sleep in safety tonight and offer him a job and a little money in exchange for his hard labor.

* * *

"I don't need any damned help," the liveryman growled. "I can't afford to pay you a cent so take that big wolf and get movin'!"

Bodie turned and headed on down the street. He'd entered two livery stables and been told both times to git. Still, he was hopeful, even though it was starting to rain hard and cold. At the Rocky Mountain Livery, footsore and weary, Bodie finally caught a break. "You a good worker, boy?"

"Yes, sir."

"You a thief?"

"No, sir."

"Well, we'll see about that. What about that dog?"

"We go together," Bodie said simply. "He won't harm any stock and he is quiet."

"Good watchdog?"

"None better."

The owner of the stables was an old, rumpled bachelor in his sixties, once large but now stooped from years of hard work. He was lean and his hands were huge.

"You eaten lately?"

"Bought some scraps for myself and Homer this morning. Nothing since."

"Well, I was just settin' down to some beans and cornbread. I cook my own inside the barn, where I got a little place to sleep and live. You can't stay there, though."

"We'd do fine in a hay pile."

"Let's get out of this rain. My name is Otis. Otis Redman. What be yours, boy?"

"Bodie."

"Last name?"

"Stock."

"Huh. Where your ma and pa be?"

"I never knew my pa, and my ma is gone or maybe in a town way out in eastern California called Bodie."

"Bodie from Bodie, huh?"

"Yes, sir."

"Well, come on in and I'll feed you and the dog. You're so thin and poor-lookin' it'd take two of you to make a shadow."

"Yes, sir."

"Come along then, Bodie. I'll get you fed and some clean horse blankets for you to dry off with and then sleep under. We can talk tomorrow morning about what I might be willin' to pay in wages."

"Thank you."

"No cause for thanks, Bodie. You'll earn your keep here or you'll soon be sent packin'."

Bodie and Homer were fed beans spiced up with chili peppers, and although Homer didn't really take well to them, he ate them anyway. Bodie thought they were real tasty, and the cornbread was still warm, and Otis had honey.

"Feelin' better now?" Otis asked when they'd cleaned the pot.

"Yes, sir."

"You're too young to be off on your own, kid. You and that dog . . . By the way, who shot or stabbed him?"

"Bad fella," Bodie said, not wanting to explain his part in a killing.

"Dog bite the man that shot him?"

"Yes he did. Homer about took his leg off."

Otis threw back his head and laughed because he thought that was real funny. When he'd finished laughing, he lit a pipe and told Bodie some long ago stories about Denver and some women that he'd loved and lost. Bodie and Homer both fell asleep listening to the lonesome old bachelor rattle on and on.

Chapter 5

"We've looked everywhere," Longarm told Gloria
that evening at the Belmont Restaurant. "I even
checked the freighting companies, along with the
railroad and stagecoach lines. No one has seen Bodie
or Homer."

"If they had, they'd have remembered," Gloria
said. "So where do you think that they're hiding?"

"I have no idea." Longarm was both baffled and
discouraged. Even worse, true to his word, Sheriff
Miller had visited his boss at the Federal Building and
raised hell about Longarm's role in the triple shooting.
He'd demanded that Longarm be stripped of his badge,
but of course Billy Vail had flatly refused. Still, it was
a problem both for Billy and the department, so Longarm desperately needed Bodie to come forward and
tell his version of the shooting.

"What happens now?" Gloria asked as she used
her fork to idly play with her salad.

"We keep looking," Longarm told her. "If Bodie hasn't left Denver, then sooner or later he'll be spotted. I've told everyone to get in touch with me the minute they see the boy and his dog. Someone will be getting in touch with me sooner rather than later."

"What a mess!" Gloria exclaimed. "And what a turnaround regarding Ida and Rose and their feelings for Bodie."

"Yes," Longarm agreed. "I think they realize that Bodie never had much of a chance to succeed in life given the erratic and irresponsible behavior of his mother all the time the boy was growing up."

"Do you think Bodie is salvageable?"

"I'm certain that he is," Longarm replied. "I was pretty wild myself when I was Bodie's age."

"But surely you must have had a far superior upbringing."

"I did," Longarm admitted. "I actually had very fine and respected parents back in West Virginia. Back when I was growing up things were pretty stable, until the War Between the States. But where Bodie was raised in the wild boom towns of Nevada and California, there would have been no stability. Probably very few schools or churches. The kid would have been hard-pressed in those places to find a good man to pattern his life after."

"I sure hope that the boy is all right." Gloria fretted. "I feel kind of responsible for his welfare and I've never even laid eyes on the boy or his dog."

"They're quite the pair," Longarm mused aloud. "Bodie and Homer are both thin as rails and ragged."

"It's storming out tonight," Gloria worried, obviously too distracted to enjoy her meal. "Do you think that they're huddling under some wagon or boardwalk trying to keep warm and dry?"

"No," Longarm answered, wanting to reassure her. "Bodie strikes me as being a survivor. He's going to know that his dog is weak from loss of blood, and he did steal those thirty dollars from Dr. Winslow. So if Bodie needed to rent a room tonight and buy something to eat for himself and for Homer, he'd have enough money to do so."

"Too bad he turned out to be a thief."

"Yeah," Longarm said, "but if you'd heard his story as I did, you'd understand that Bodie is a kid that will do whatever he has to do to take care of himself and that wolf dog."

"I wish that I could help you look for him, but I've got the shop to see after."

"I know and that's fine. I'm very sure that within a few days, if Bodie and Homer don't decide to leave town in the dead of night, we'll get a sighting. And when we do, I'll make sure that Bodie doesn't get away from me again."

"Sounds like Ida and Rose might like to take him into their beautiful home."

"Maybe," Longarm said, not too sure if the pair of women really understood the enormity of taking in a boy and his dog that were so independent, undisciplined, and headstrong.

Longarm and Gloria went back to his place and made love, but their deep concern about Bodie's welfare and whereabouts meant that their lovemaking was more restrained. Gloria was still highly aroused, as was Longarm, but neither of them seemed up to a bout of wild and frequent lovemaking like the one they'd experienced the night before.

In the morning, Longarm headed for work, and when he entered Marshal Billy Vail's office, he was told to close the door behind him so that they could speak in private. Billy came right to the point. "Custis, I'm getting a lot of grief and pressure from Sheriff Miller, who swears that you've been derelict in your duty. He says that you haven't even come by his office to file a formal report on the shootings."

"He's right," Longarm confessed. "I've been so busy hunting for Bodie that I just haven't taken the time."

"Well, do it as soon as you leave this office," Billy suggested. "We're feds, and we have enough trouble dealing with the local authorities without you rubbing the sheriff the wrong way."

"He's worthless and isn't going to get reelected. In a couple of months Clyde Miller will be just a bad and fading memory."

"That is probably true," Billy agreed, "but even so I'd like to be able to say that we kept our end of the bargain when it came to being cooperative."

"I'll go see him right away," Longarm promised.

"So where do you think this kid has gone?"

"I don't know. Bodie could have left Denver, but I don't think so."

"Why not?"

Longarm shrugged his broad shoulders. "Just a hunch. I believe that Bodie really wanted to see his grandmother and aunt. And I think he'll do that before he leaves town."

"Are they aware that the kid might pay them a sudden and unexpected visit?"

"They are."

Billy frowned. "I've heard rumors that the grandmother, Mrs. Ida Clark, is in very poor health. A boy with blood on his hands might be enough of a shock to put her in the ground."

"I know." Longarm came to his feet. "Billy, I've been everywhere and I've told everyone that they need to let me know the minute they spot the boy and his dog. Trust me . . . they both stand out and will show up in a day or two at the most."

"I do trust you, Custis. And you need to file a report in my office regarding your role in the shootings. Have you done that yet?"

"No."

"Then please do so before you go to visit Sheriff Miller."

"Okay," Longarm said, hating any kind of paperwork.

Billy Vail suddenly relaxed. "Custis, it may cheer you up a bit to know that I've learned that the pair of men involved in the shootings were hardened criminals. They'd been in and out of Nevada, Arizona, and Colorado prisons for years. I don't know a thing about the late John Stock, but I suspect he was simply a random victim and that the kid and the dog were caught up in the gunfire. However, I still find it hard to understand how a boy that young could shove a derringer into someone's chest and pull the trigger.

I'll try to reserve my judgment until after I've read your report and talked to the boy."

"I was there, and after watching what happened to John Stock, it isn't so hard to understand. If you'd also seen it, you would have done exactly what Bodie did . . . kill the son of a bitch."

"All right," Billy said quietly. "Write your report and then go and do whatever you have to do to smooth Sheriff Miller's feathers."

"I absolutely can't abide that man."

"Neither can I," Billy replied, "but as you said, he isn't going to be reelected, so just do what I'm asking."

"Okay."

Longarm left the office and went to his desk. There were three other deputies in their small offices, and all of them nodded in greeting but were wise enough not to pester him with questions about the shootings. Longarm sat down at his desk, picked up his pen, and began to write out the official office report. Finished, he read over his words, decided that they were adequate, left the report with a secretary and then headed for Sheriff Miller's office.

"So," the sheriff said when Longarm walked in, "you've finally decided to pay me a visit. What a big fucking honor!"

"Cut the bullshit."

Longarm didn't wait to be invited to sit and pulled up a chair, while noting that the other two deputies in the office were now all ears. "What do you need to know from me?"

Miller's contemptuous smile faded. "I want to know *everything*. And after I've heard your version of the shootings, I'll decide if I'm going to arrest you or not."

"Arrest me?" Longarm asked with genuine amazement.

"Yeah."

Longarm laughed, and it wasn't a nice sound. "Sheriff, if you're really dumb enough to try to arrest me, you will either wind up in the hospital or the morgue. Do I make myself clear?"

Miller's beefy face turned scarlet red and he nearly choked with anger. Finally, he gained control of himself and managed to say, "Just give me all the damned facts."

Longarm spent the next ten minutes telling the sheriff and his two nosy deputies exactly what had happened out on Colfax. He omitted nothing but did not go into any great detail. When he was finished, he didn't wait to answer questions but came to his feet and headed for the door.

"I'm not through with you!" Sheriff Miller yelled.

"Yes you are," Longarm called back over his shoulder.

"I want that boy in my custody!"

"Can't find him right now," Longarm said, turning back with a cold smile.

"Custis, if you're hiding him for some gawdamn reason, I'll have your balls sliced off and fed to the hogs."

"If you don't stop threatening me and my job, I'm going to kick your fat ass up between your shoulder blades right here in front of your two worthless deputies."

Miller's jaw dropped, and his deputies, probably feeling they had to make some kind of show of loyalty, came out of their chairs and moved toward Longarm as if they were going to give him a fight.

"Don't even think about it," Longarm warned, his words bringing the pair to a standstill.

Longarm turned and headed out into the street. He'd looked everywhere he could think of for Bodie yesterday, and now he had to think of some new places that the kid and his dog might be hiding. For the sake of Bodie's welfare and immediate future, he needed to find the kid before Sheriff Miller, or else the boy would be caught up in a legal and jurisdictional situation from which he might never recover.

Chapter 6

Two frustrating days later, Custis stepped out of the barbershop and heard his named being called. "Marshal Long!"

He turned to see the mortician, Mr. Dudley Swilling, rushing across the street. Longarm immediately figured that Swilling wanted money for his services and perhaps considered that the big federal marshal had some responsibility for the cost of burying at least one of the three men.

"I've been looking for you," the mortician said, catching his breath. Swilling was a tall and older man, always somber-faced and looking as if he had just lost his best friend; Longarm suspected that was because Swilling had been an undertaker all his adult life. He was bent and thin and always outfitted for his professional duties with a worn black coat, white shirt, black pants shiny with age, and unpolished shoes. Swilling usually wore a black derby that was ten years out of

style, but today that was missing and Longarm realized the man was almost completely bald.

"Hell, Mr. Swilling," Longarm said with resigna-
tion. "Have the three men been buried?"

"Of course. And I was wondering if we might have
a few words in private."

Longarm knew that Swilling would hound him
until he agreed to talk, so he said, "And that would
most likely be about your compensation?"

"Yes, that and more."

Longarm was irritable after searching two days
for Bodie and having nothing to show for it. "I'm
pretty busy, Mr. Swilling, but we can talk for a moment. Let's just walk over here where we can speak
privately."

"Good idea," the undertaker agreed, following
Longarm to a place beside a horse trough where no
one passing by would overhear their conversation.

"I have something very important for you," Swilling said, removing a thick envelope from an inside
coat pocket.

"Don't tell me that you are presenting me with a
bill for your services, because I'm not paying it. The
city—"

"Marshal, that's *not* what I'm here for," Swilling
interrupted. "I've long had a formal agreement with
Denver that insures they will reimburse me twenty-
five dollars for every deceased indigent person I pre-
pare to have buried. Twenty-five dollars gets the
deceased a cheap pine box, no flowers or service, and
not even a headstone, but instead a cheap wooden
cross on which I have a man carve the deceased name

and date of birth and death, if they are available. Nameless paupers are buried in the paupers' untended section of the cemetery, and no one will likely ever visit their graves."

"I see." Longarm looked down at the envelope in Swilling's hand with more than a little curiosity. "What is this?"

"It's a letter that I assume is from that boy's mother. I found it on the body of John Stock. I took the liberty of reading it and I think you should do likewise."

"Why?"

"When you read the letter you'll immediately understand, and there are also a few valuable possessions included in that envelope."

"All right," Longarm said. "I'm looking for Bodie and having no luck at all. But sooner or later I'll find the boy and deliver this envelope. Is there any money to be passed on to Bodie?"

"Very little cash, but there are a few small gold nuggets that should bring the orphan several hundred dollars. There is also a woman's gold locket, with what I assume is a cameo of the boy's mother inside, along with a diamond ring and necklace."

Longarm was stunned. "*Real* diamonds?"

"I'm not a jeweler, but yes, I'd say the diamonds are real and their value is considerable."

"That's pretty hard to believe."

"And why is that?"

"Because Bodie led me to believe that his mother was always facing hard circumstances. And as you could see from the dress and appearance of the dead man, John Stock, he looked to be in equally bad straits. So, Mr. Swilling, I'm confused as to why Mr. Stock would have anything of real value on his person."

"I understand your confusion," the mortician said. "The man's shoes were worn out, as was his clothing. He had no watch and, as I said, very little cash. But it is the letter that will really set your head to spinning."

"Letter?"

"Yes. But before you open and read it, I should warn you that it will be very upsetting . . . even to someone as accustomed to murder and treachery as you are in your dangerous line of work."

"Thanks," Longarm said, very distracted by what he'd just been told. "Was there anything else of value or interest on Mr. Stock's body?"

"No." Swilling hesitated. "But, if I may be so bold as to suggest, I really hope that you or someone will offer up a modest remuneration in order that John Stock at least be given a modest marble headstone. One with his name and date of death. The wooden crosses last only a few years, but even a small marble headstone will last for the ages."

"You just said that no one ever visits the paupers' section of our Denver cemetery."

"That's true, but the boy might want to visit his stepfather's grave someday. And by the way, I saw the boy this morning."

"You did!"

"Yes, he was shoveling manure and feeding horses at the Rocky Mountain Livery. I know the man that he works for, Otis Redman, and he is a good person. I buried his wife over ten years ago, so you may rest assured that the boy is being taken care of and not being abused or mistreated."

"I should have guessed that would be the only kind of place that Bodie would go to find work and to keep his dog."

"The dog was in plain sight. I walked past the livery and it barked a time or two but didn't act aggressive."

"Thank you so much for telling me where to find Bodie," Longarm said earnestly. "I've been searching everywhere for him and we were worried."

"I hope," Swilling said, "that you don't let our sadistic and cruel Sheriff Miller get his hands on that boy."

"Not a chance." Longarm turned his attention back to the envelope in his hand. "Why would you say that Bodie might someday want to visit John Stock's grave?"

"Well, if for no other reason than to *piss* upon it."

Longarm's jaw dropped, but before he could respond, Mortician Swilling was hurrying on down the street.

Longarm found a nearby park bench and opened a small, clean, and white envelope which contained a bloodstained page of expensive stationery. Longarm took a deep breath and read these words:

My dear son Bodie,

I know that I have always been a terrible mother and for that I am most sorry. What you do not know is that after John took you away from me I went to the Comstock Lode where I changed my profession and found salvation. This changed my life and I soon met a Mr. Burlington. I told him about you and about my wicked, sinful past, but he loved and forgave me and we were married. Mr. Burlington is quite wealthy and I am hoping that this letter will find its way into your hands and that you will come quickly to Virginia City where I now live in a fine mansion. Mr. Burlington has agreed to take you in and he will be good to you. Please come as soon as possible.

Your saved and repentant mother,
Mrs. Ruby Burlington

Longarm stared at the letter and then at the bloodstains for a long, long time. He tipped the envelope up and the jewelry tumbled into his hands. Mortician Swilling had been right; the jewelry was both valuable and beautiful.

Suddenly, Longarm had a million questions to ask, but the only man who could possibly answer them was John Stock, and he was resting in a cheap pine coffin and already rotting away in a freshly dug grave.

Chapter 7

Longarm was only a block away from the Federal Building, and before he went to collect Bodie, he thought it a good idea to see what his boss, Billy Vail, would have to say about the mysterious and blood-stained letter from the kid's mother.

"Custis," Billy said, looking up suddenly from some paperwork on his desk. "I just read your report and it is lacking in some pertinent details."

"I've got something very important for you to read," Longarm said, taking a seat in front of the man's desk.

"How important?"

"That's what I want you to help me decide."

"I don't like guessing games," Billy said. "What is it you are talking about?"

"This," Longarm said, producing the envelope with the letter and the jewelry. "The mortician, Mr.

Dudley Swilling, found me on the street and gave me what he discovered on the body of John Stock."

Billy poured the jewelry out onto his desk and his eyes widened with surprise. He glanced up at Longarm and said, "I thought you told me that the boy's father was ragged and undoubtedly dead broke."

"That's what I told you, but I obviously missed a few things," Longarm replied. "Now before you ask me any more questions, I suggest you read the letter."

"My gawd! The letter itself is badly stained with blood!" Billy frowned with confusion. "John Stock's blood, I assume?"

"I don't think so," Longarm answered. "The envelope that contained the letter is clean without a trace of blood."

"I don't understand this."

"Neither do I, but I'm beginning to form some ideas. Just read the letter, Billy."

Billy read the letter twice, and then he carefully laid it down before him and studied it for several moments. "All right, what do you think?"

"I believe that Ruby Burlington wrote the letter and asked John Stock to deliver it to Bodie. But when Stock saw and understood what the letter meant, he must have flown into a rage and murdered Bodie's mother. Then, he stripped her of her jewelry and hurried off to the town of Bodie to collect the boy. Only instead of taking him to Virginia City, he brought him to Denver."

Billy leaned back in his leather desk chair, steepled his stubby fingers, and said, "That's quite a theory, Custis. But how on earth could you come up with it?"

"Think about it," Longarm urged. "If John Stock murdered and robbed Ruby Burlington, he would have had to run for his life. And when he was doing that, I think he remembered that Ruby's wealthy mother lived here in Denver. So it's an easy leap to imagine that John Stock would bring Bodie here and spin some wild story about Ruby being murdered. He'd gain Ida Clark's sympathy. The dear old woman wouldn't have any idea that her wild daughter had found religion and married a wealthy man. Ida Clark would have taken John Stock and Bodie into her home, and he could have then robbed and perhaps even murdered Ida and Rose. Then, he would have amassed a small fortune in stolen jewelry and money and lit out for parts unknown."

"I see what you're thinking and you may just have it," Billy said, chin dipping up and down. "John Stock would have been taken into Ida Clark's fine home because of Bodie. And he would have claimed this bloodstained letter had been given to him by the authorities in Virginia City so he'd have the proof of her murder."

"Exactly."

Billy clucked his tongue. "So what do you think we ought to do now?"

"The last thing we want to do is to tell Sheriff Miller about this or give him any evidence. He'd go straight to the press and try to make himself look as if he'd solved some murder case, and he'd want Bodie completely out of the picture."

"But we've lost the boy."

"Mr. Swilling found him, and Bodie is working at the Rocky Mountain Stable."

"Then we must get him before the sheriff or one of his deputies chances upon Bodie and takes him into custody."

"Exactly."

"But then what?"

Longarm shook his head. "There is something else that has occurred to me."

"I'm all ears."

"What if the two men that murdered John Stock on Colfax Avenue weren't just randomly picking out their victim?"

"What do you mean?"

"What I mean," Longarm said, "is that you told me they were seasoned and lifetime criminals. So why would they attack a ragged man and a boy? If they were going to take the risk of robbing anyone, wouldn't they have picked someone that at least appeared to be prosperous?"

"Yes," Billy said, "that makes sense. But . . ."

"What I'm suggesting," Longarm said, "is that the murder of John Stock wasn't random at all. That the two men who attacked him knew John Stock and his plan and followed him from the Comstock Lode intent on somehow cashing in on his scheme."

"Custis, that's quite a stretch!"

"Is it really?" Longarm asked. "What other possible reason could there be for all this evidence and what happened? Surely you must agree that if I'm right, everything that has happened makes some sense."

"Yes, but how would you ever know if Mrs. Burlington was robbed and murdered?"

"We could send a telegram to the sheriff in Reno and ask him to see that it was received by whoever is in charge up on the Comstock Lode."

"That seems to be to be unwise."

"I agree. Until we really know if Ruby Burlington is alive or dead—and the same goes for her wealthy husband—we can't afford to tip our hand."

"Are you telling me that you have to go to Virginia City and get to the bottom of this?"

"That's exactly what I'm telling you," Longarm said.

"This isn't a *federal* case."

"I know that, but Bodie's very life may be at stake. Who is to say that the mastermind of this whole murder thing didn't *hire* John Stock and perhaps even paid him to kill wealthy Mr. Burlington."

"You're posing a lot of what-ifs," Billy said.

"I know that," Longarm confessed. "But what I'm thinking is that John Stock and the two other men who were shot down on Colfax might be just the tip of a murderous plan. The real money—if this letter is accurate, and we have the jewelry to see that it is—might be the brains behind a plot to rob and murder Mr. Burlington, then steal all his assets."

Billy looked up at the ceiling. "So we collect Bodie and . . ."

"I'm not sure of what to do with him," Longarm

said, "and I'd not want to tell him what we think might have happened to his mother and her husband."

"We can't withhold all this from the boy if his mother has been murdered."

"We can until we know for certain exactly what is going on in Virginia City," Longarm argued.

Billy scowled. "I can't authorize travel money for something like this."

"Then don't," Longarm said. "I'll go on my own because I have to."

"There is a small matter of official business that you could check on in Reno," Billy offered. "That way I could authorize travel money."

"Then do it," Longarm said. "Because I'm going to go get Bodie and then I'm heading off to Virginia City."

"Very well," Billy said quietly as his forefinger stroked the bloodstained letter. "And frankly, I couldn't live with this bloody mystery for the rest of my life."

"And neither could I," Longarm told his boss. "It's just something that would eat at us for the remainder of our days."

"Go then," Billy ordered. "I'll have money for you this afternoon. You can be on the train first thing tomorrow morning."

"Thanks, Billy."

"In the meantime, I'll keep this envelope with the letter and jewelry in a safe deposit box at the bank. When our investigation is over, we'll see that Bodie gets everything, Custis, just make certain that the boy is safe."

"I will. And his dog too."

Billy managed a smile. "Oh, I'd forgotten about the dog. Sure. Both the boy and the dog."

With nothing left to say, Longarm headed for the door.

Chapter 8

Before heading over to the Rocky Mountain Livery,
Longarm made a quick stop to see Gloria Harmon at
her shop. He knew that she was as worried as anyone
about Bodie, and he felt that he ought to bring her up
to date, which he did in as few words as possible.

"Thank heavens you've found him!" Gloria said
with a huge sigh of relief. "I was beginning to think
the worst . . . you know, that he'd been badly injured
or murdered."

"No, the mortician said that the man he is working
for, a Mr. Otis Redman, is a good person. I'm sure
that Bodie is getting along fine, and his dog Homer
was with him."

"So what are we going to do now?"

"What's the 'we' stuff?" Longarm asked. "This
is my job and I'm going to go see Bodie."

"What if he won't come with you?"

Longarm's brow furrowed. "I was thinking about

that on the way over here from the Federal Building,
and I have to say there's a good chance Bodie isn't
going to cooperate."

"You can't just grab him by the collar and drag him
away from that livery."

"I know. But I think I can persuade him that his
life could get very unpleasant if Sheriff Miller or one
of his deputies latches onto him."

"I could close up shop and come with you."

"No," Longarm told her. "I think I simply need to
have a quiet talk with Bodie. Tell him the facts and
then see how he reacts. The kid is smart, and the last
thing he'll want is for the sheriff to take him into
custody and away from his dog."

"Good luck," Gloria offered as a customer entered
her shop.

"Thanks."

Longarm headed for the livery located on nearby
Federal Street. He wondered how Bodie would react
when they met and decided there was just no way to
predict how the kid would take his sudden appearance.

Ten minutes later, Longarm rounded a corner and
saw the livery. He walked directly into the big barn,
and there was Bodie sitting on a bale of straw drinking a cup of water, with Homer resting at his feet.

"Hello, Bodie."

The boy showed no reaction at all.

"How is your dog doing?"

"He's on the mend," Bodie replied.

"We need to talk."

"I expected you would be around sooner or later," Bodie said. "But before you say anything, I'm not going anywhere with you and neither is Homer."

Longarm nodded with understanding. "Sheriff Miller and his deputies are searching high and low for you. If the sheriff gets you, he'll put you into custody and you won't be able to keep Homer."

"*Nobody* is separating me from Homer," Bodie said, face tightening. "And I'm doin' just fine. All I want is to be left alone."

"I wish you could be left alone," Longarm said, "but I'm afraid that isn't possible. And I've got some things to tell you."

"About what?"

"About John Stock . . . and your mother."

At the mention of his mother, Bodie jumped to his feet, eyes hardening. "What do you know about her?"

"Take it easy," Longarm said.

"Any trouble here, Bodie?" a voice called out from the gloom in the back of the barn.

"No, sir! I'm talking to the law. Ain't no trouble."

The old liveryman emerged from the shadows, took one look at Custis, and then turned around and disappeared out the big back door.

"What about my mother?" Bodie asked. "Or are you just sayin' something to trick me into doing what you want?"

Longarm sat down on a nearby bale of straw and took a moment to compose his words. "John Stock had a letter that was found on his body. It was a letter from your mother, and she has remarried and is living in Virginia City on the Comstock. The letter was asking you to come live with her and her new husband, whose name is Mr. Burlington."

The half-filled cup of water spilled from Bodie's hand, but he didn't seem to notice. "My ma got married again?"

"That's right," Longarm answered. "The letter says that she found religion, fell in love, and married a pretty good and wealthy man. Both she and her new husband want you to come and live with them in Virginia City."

Bodie looked away for a moment, then turned back to Longarm and said, "I don't believe you."

"It's true."

"Show me the letter."

"Could you read it if I did?"

"Not much of it . . . but some. I'd recognize her handwriting in a second, though."

"The letter is in the hands of my boss. And, Bodie, there's something else you need to know. The letter is bloodstained."

Even in the dim light of the barn's interior, Longarm saw the boy pale. He whispered, "Go on."

"I'm pretty sure that your onetime stepfather, John Stock, murdered or badly injured your mother and stole her jewelry. Most likely, he intended to take you to your grandmother and aunt and tell them some tall tale about how your mother died and he was the one that helped you get to Denver and safety. John Stock would have hung around your grandmother's place a few days . . . or even weeks, playing on her sympathy, and then he'd have robbed and possibly even murdered her and your aunt just like he might have done your mother."

Bodie was silent a long time before he said, "I still don't believe a word of it."

"It's sad but true."

"I need to see the letter."

Longarm scowled. "The letter is addressed to you, Bodie. And I've no doubt that you'll recognize the handwriting."

"I want to see it now!"

Longarm decided that he had no choice. "All right. Let's go to my office, and I'll talk my boss into showing you the letter and the jewelry."

"Why would my ma send me jewelry?"

"She didn't," Longarm explained. "John Stock took it away from her, probably after he killed her. But I won't know that until I'm in Virginia City."

"You're goin' there?"

"I am," Longarm said. "I'm leaving on the train tomorrow. It runs up to Cheyenne and then all the way to Reno. I can catch a coach from Reno to Virginia City."

"I'm goin' with you."

"No."

"I'm goin' with or without you, Marshal. And I'm takin' my dog."

"It's a long, long way to the Comstock Lode."

"I know. I come from Bodie. I know how far it is, but I'll get there."

"Your grandmother, Ida, and aunt Rose would like you to live with them. They have a fine house. You and Homer could stay with them, and when

I get back with some answers, we could decide what to do."

"Is Sheriff Miller that dumb that he couldn't even find me there?"

Longarm almost smiled. "He's dumb, but you're right. He'd find you at your grandmother's house."

"Well then? I ain't never rode a train and neither has Homer."

"You can't take him on the train."

"I'll take him or not go."

"You can't take a dog on the train."

"I can if I sleep in a cattle or freight car. Some of them go to Reno, don't they?"

"Yes, but . . ."

"Well that's it then. If you got the letter and it's from my ma, I'm goin' to Virginia City one damned way or the other."

Longarm had to admire the boy's determination. "Let's go to my office and see what my boss says."

"I don't give a damn what your boss says," Bodie told him. "That letter and that jewelry you said belonged to my ma now belong to me. I could sell the jewelry and have enough money to buy my own damn ticket to Reno, couldn't I?"

"I suppose."

"Anything else that my ma had for me?"

"A few gold nuggets."

"Well then I'm set for money, and I'm leavin' with or without you, Marshal."

"Were you born this stubborn?" Longarm asked.

"I was born hard and I stayed hard," Bodie said without a trace of pride. "I been on the bottom, and

I'm sick and tired of it. Don't like being told what to do."

"Then how do you even hold a job like this?" Longarm asked, looking around.

"I ain't been here but a couple of days. Mr. Redman, he don't tell me what to do like I was some slave. He asks me to do things and I do 'em because he asks. That's all it takes, just the askin' rather than the tellin'. Understand?"

"I understand."

"Okay, then. I'll go with you if you ask."

"Would you go with me to my office to see that letter your mother wrote, maybe even on the day she was murdered?"

"Yes, sir, I will. But Homer comes with me."

"Fine," Longarm said. "Let's go."

"Wait a minute."

Longarm watched Bodie go out the back of the barn. He was gone only a few minutes, and Longarm figured it was to tell Otis Redman that he was leaving for the Comstock Lode and to thank him for his help.

Bodie was a good kid. Hard as nails, but a good kid all the same. Longarm wasn't sure if Billy Vail would go along with letting Bodie go off to Virginia City. But then again, Longarm didn't think that Billy had any choice in the matter. None at all.

Chapter 9

"So," Billy Vail said when Custis and Bodie walked into his office, "you've been found."

"I wasn't lost," Bodie said. "I had a good stable job and the marshal decided that was over."

Billy's eyes moved to the huge dog. "Custis, you know you can't bring that beast into the Federal Building."

"I know, but I promised Bodie that they could stay together. It was that or else arrest and then drag him here."

"I came for the letter my ma wrote me," Bodie declared. "And I guess there was some jewelry worth a lot of money."

"That's right."

Bodie stepped right up to Billy's desk. "I don't have much of anything other than Homer and what I'm wearin'. So if you have something of mine, I'd be obliged to have it now."

Billy studied the ragged and dirty kid. "All right, but first you're going to have to answer some questions, and I want you to be honest. If I think you're lying to me or to Custis, I won't give you the letter or the jewelry. Understand?"

Bodie nodded, lips tightly compressed.

"Both of you have a seat and close the door behind you."

When everyone was seated, Billy said, "Bodie, when was the last time you saw your mother?"

"A couple of years ago."

"And at that time was she living with John Stock, the man who was shot to death and claimed to be your stepfather?"

"Nope. They'd separated."

"How long ago?"

"I was around twelve."

"Do you know why your mother left you with Mr. Stock?"

"She was havin' a real hard time makin' a livin'. Said she was goin' to a town called Eureka and she'd send for me when she had some money saved and a place for us."

"But she never did."

"No. I lived and worked doin' just what I'm doin' now. Muckin' out stalls, feedin' and groomin' horses. Shovelin' a lot of horse shit. Cleaning spittoons and sweeping out saloons."

"Why did you come to Denver?"

Bodie drew a deep breath. "John said I had a rich granny and aunt. He said they'd give us a place to stay, a little work and some money. He said we'd both wear new clothes and eat well. It sounded fine to me, and I'd lost track of Ma, so I came."

"Had you ever seen the two men that attacked you and your stepfather out on the street?"

Bodie looked down at his worn-out shoes. He reached down and petted his dog. "I might have seen 'em in Bodie," he finally admitted. "They looked like some men that I'd seen there, but I can't be sure."

"Did they say anything to John Stock before they attacked and killed him?"

"Nope. But . . ."

"But what?" Longarm pressed.

"Well, when John saw those two big men, he turned and I thought he was goin' to run. But then he whirled back, and that's when the one killed him and I picked up the derringer and finished the fight."

"So," Longarm mused, "John Stock *did* know those men."

"I kind of thought he did," Bodie said. "I never saw a man go so pale as when those two rounded a corner and came face-to-face with us. Now, can I have that letter?"

Billy nodded. "All right. Would you like me to read it out loud for you?"

"I want to see it first. See if it looks like it was written by my ma."

Billy reached into his drawer, drew out the envelope, and then handed it to Bodie. When the kid extracted the letter and saw the bloodstains, his face turned pale. He stared at the letter and looked over the words for a long time and then whispered, "This was writ by my ma."

"Bodie," Longarm said, "it doesn't mean for sure that your mother is dead."

"No," Bodie grated, "but it sure seems to be that way."

"That's why I have to go to Virginia City," Longarm announced. He looked to Billy. "Bodie says he is also determined to go to Virginia City."

"That would be very unwise."

"I know," Longarm agreed. "But you're going to have to put him behind bars or he'll run away and eventually end up on the Comstock Lode. It'd be far better for Billy to accompany me than to go back on his own."

"It's a long way to Virginia City," Bodie offered. "But one way or another, me and Homer would find a way to get there."

"Yeah," Billy Vail said, "I'm sure that you would . . . eventually. Now, let me read the letter out loud."

Billy read the letter while Custis studied the kid's face for any clues as to his inner emotions. Despite his young age, Bodie remained stone-faced, barely breathing until the letter was finished and handed back to him.

"Where is Ma's jewelry?" Bodie managed to ask, his voice barely louder than a whisper.

Billy reached into his drawer and brought out the ring and necklace along with the small gold nuggets. "Did you ever hear of this Mr. Burlington?"

"No."

"Then your mother must have met him after she left you. Did you even know that she had gone to Virginia City and gotten religion?"

"Nope. She disappeared like smoke in wind," Bodie said. "But if she's been killed, then I'm glad that she made her peace with God before it happened. And that she had some happiness and love right at the end."

Tears began to roll down Bodie's dusty cheeks.

"I think," Longarm said, "I'll take Bodie over to meet his grandmother Ida and aunt Rose. He'll probably stay with them tonight."

"If they'll put up with my dog."

"Yes, if they'll do that. And in the morning I'll buy two train tickets to Reno."

Billy's expression was dark. "Bodie, you know that if there is something bad going on in Virginia City, you could be putting yourself into serious danger. It could even get you killed."

"Why would anyone want to kill me?"

"If your mother married a wealthy man, then you might be a primary benefactor."

"Speak plain English," Bodie demanded.

"What he meant to say," Longarm added, "is that the reason those two big men suddenly showed up is that they were sent to kill John Stock and very possibly you as well. That way, if you had stood to inherit anything, you'd be permanently eliminated."

Bodie considered this for a moment. "I don't expect anyone left me much money."

"Well," Longarm countered, "you'd never have expected to be holding a diamond ring and necklace and some gold nuggets, now would you?"

"No sir."

"What I'm trying to tell you," Longarm continued,

"is that there could be a lot of money in a will and you could be killed for it."

"I'll sell this jewelry and buy a new gun and repeating rifle," Bodie told them. "And I'll learn to shoot fast and straight."

"Custis, this is getting worse by the minute. Take Bodie over to see his grandmother and aunt, then come back and I'll have your ticket and travel money ready. But you'll have to check in on that little matter in Reno I spoke to you earlier about."

"Sure, but what about *Bodie's* ticket and expenses?"

"If Mrs. Ida Clark won't pay for it, then Bodie sells the jewelry and buys his own ticket. I'm just not sure how you're going to talk the railroad into letting him take the dog."

"I'll figure out something," Longarm promised.

"I'm sure you will."

Billy shook Bodie's hand, saying, "I hope you find out that your mother is alive and doing well."

"That's not too likely."

"Probably not, but I want to wish you good luck, Bodie. It's going to be helpful to have you leave Denver before Sheriff Miller gets his hooks into you. If that happened, we'd have a serious problem."

Bodie nodded with understanding.

Longarm walked Bodie and Homer over to Center Street, thinking he should have cleaned and dressed the kid up a little before meeting his grandmother and aunt. But Bodie probably wouldn't have stood for being cleaned up and made to look respectable; too bad that the boy and the dog stunk so bad.

Longarm just hoped that the two women on Center Street would not think the pair disgusting and refuse to take them into their home.

"What are they like?" Bodie suddenly asked as they approached the yellow house.

"They're very kind."

"Judging from the house, they must be rich."

"Maybe not rich," Longarm said, "but comfortable."

"Rich," Bodie insisted. "If you live in a big house like that, you gotta be rich. They have anyone else livin' with 'em?"

"Not that I know of."

Bodie glanced at Homer. "No dogs or cats?"

"I don't think so."

"Good. Homer don't much care for either. It would go real bad if my dog ate any of their pets."

"Yeah."

"What the hell am I supposed to say to 'em?"

"Whatever you want to say, only don't cuss. These are ladies."

"Sure. Do I tell 'em about the letter I got from ma with the bloodstains?"

"You can if you want, but I don't think it would be a very good idea."

"Maybe not. Might be too much for real ladies to take on top of everything."

"That's right."

"Let's just get this over with," Bodie said quietly as he started toward the fine yellow house.

Chapter 10

"Mrs. Clark, this is your grandson," Longarm said as he and the kid stood on the front porch. "And that's his dog, Homer."

Ida and Rose took involuntary steps backward, clearly shocked. Rose broke an awkward silence by saying, "Bodie, it's a pleasure to meet you and . . . and your dog."

"Yes," Ida blurted, recovering quickly. "We've heard quite a lot about you."

"Probably none of it good," Bodie said, taking off his battered felt hat and wringing the brim in his dirty hands. "I come from a long way off and things ain't been too easy for me in Denver."

"We've heard about your troubles," Rose said. "And we'd like to help you out."

"Not much you can do for me and Homer except feed us. We can't be here for long."

"Oh," Ida said, "and why is that?"

"Tomorrow me and the marshal are goin' to get on a train and ride all the way to Reno, then take a stage or a wagon on to Virginia City. I'm going to find out if my mother is still alive or not . . . but it don't look too promising."

Ida's hand fluttered to her mouth and she looked away for a moment, struggling to gain her composure. Longarm touched her on the arm and said, "Bodie means that his mother wasn't feeling too well the last time he saw her."

"I see," Ida managed to say. "Bodie, we would like to help you out in any way that we can."

"A good meal for me and Homer and some cash would be appreciated, ma'am."

"Of course," Rose said quickly. "Would you please come inside and make yourselves comfortable. Ida and I have made some freshly squeezed lemonade."

"That would be nice," Longarm said, wishing he were someplace else.

Bodie told his dog to wait on the front porch, and once inside the house he was obviously impressed. "You sure have a nice place here," he told the two women. "Nicer than anything I've ever seen before."

"We like it, and we have an extra bedroom all made up and ready for you . . . of course, after you've had a bath and tried on some new clothes that we bought."

"You bought *me* new clothes?"

"That's right. The man at the store had seen you in the street, so he had a good idea of your size. I hope you like what we've bought for you, Bodie."

"Anything would be nicer'n what I'm wearin' now, ma'am."

* * *

An hour later, Bodie was getting along just fine with the ladies. He'd talked them into giving his dog a hambone and some scraps, and he'd taken a bath and put on the new clothes, which fit well. With his clean face and hands and his hair slicked down, the boy looked almost handsome, and Longarm could see that he was quite the talker as he told his grandmother and aunt, without being too graphic, all about the wild mining camps he'd been brought up in. Nothing was said about the shoot-out and his role in it, and for that Longarm was grateful.

When Rose led Bodie to a bedroom that had been prepared just for the kid, Longarm took a moment to speak privately to Ida.

"What do you think?"

"I can see a lot of my daughter in that boy," Ida said quietly. "And I see a lot of sadness, too."

"Bodie has had a hard life," Longarm reminded the older woman. "He looks like a boy, but he already thinks like a man. He's had to grow up very fast."

"Why are you taking him back to Nevada?" Ida asked. "Hasn't he seen enough of all that?"

"It's complicated, but necessary," Longarm assured her. "You see, there was a letter that was found on John Stock's body, and it told us some very good things and some very troubling things about Bodie's mother."

"I can't take any more strain right now," Ida confessed. "So just tell me the good things."

"Your daughter found religion and quit her wild and dangerous life to marry a good and respectable man named Mr. Burlington. Apparently, they were very much in love and Mr. Burlington was quite wealthy."

Ida took a deep breath and smiled. "That's a miracle! Whatever could be bad about something like that?"

"I'm not sure that anything is," Longarm said, unwilling to tell her about the bloodstains on the letter. "But Bodie has to go back to see his mother and meet her new husband."

"Then we will probably never see the boy again."

"Again," Longarm hedged, "I'm not sure. All I know is that Bodie needs to go with me to Virginia City. He has some questions, and I have a few of my own, which have to do with the shooting we were involved in downtown."

"I see."

Ida did not see, but Longarm knew she was trying to be understanding. "Mrs. Clark, I'll take good care of your grandson. If he wants to come back here to see you again, I'll make sure that he can."

"Very well," Ida told him. "The moment I looked into his eyes I knew that he belonged with family. If his mother is finally willing to take care of Bodie, I'm grateful. But I'm also very doubtful that is going to happen."

"And why do you say that?"

"A leopard never changes its spots, or a tiger its stripes. Ruby was always a disappointment, and I'll not allow myself to be disappointed by her ever again, so make sure that you do not leave Bodie in the hands of someone who will not remain steadfast and responsible."

"I understand, Mrs. Clark, and I share your

concern," Longarm told the woman. "Believe me, I'll
not leave the boy with his mother unless I'm absolutely certain it is in his best interest."

"Thank you," Ida said. "Thank you for that and
for bringing him to our home, even if it is only for
this one night."

"Is the dog all right staying with Bodie in his
room?"

"Oh yes, but I would rather he had brought a
smaller animal. A rabbit or a pet mouse or something
of that sort. Or a bird, perhaps."

"Yes," Longarm said, "that would have been easier.
And now, if you'll excuse me, I've got to be leaving."

"You're not staying for supper?"

"I have things to do in preparation for our trip
tomorrow," Longarm told her.

"I understand."

"I'll be by to pick up Bodie about eight o'clock
tomorrow morning."

"I'll give him enough money to purchase a round-
trip ticket."

"Do that," Longarm said on his way out the door.

That night Longarm slept again with Gloria, and
they shared a more relaxed and entertaining session of
lovemaking. In the morning, Longarm kissed her good-
bye and promised he'd return as soon as possible.

"Just be careful," she told him. "And I'll be
waiting."

Longarm then walked over to Center Street, collected
Bodie and his big dog, and together they headed for
the train station.

"I suppose you're curious about riding a train," Longarm said.

"Sure am."

"You'll like it," Longarm promised. "We'll buy you a ticket and settle in right away. This Denver Pacific train will take us up to Cheyenne, and then we'll catch the Union Pacific, which will take us all the way to Reno."

"How long will it take?"

"A little less than three days."

"Then a half day up to Virginia City."

"That's about right," Longarm told the boy as they went into the station to buy Bodie a ticket.

"Uh-oh," Longarm said. "I think we've got trouble."

Longarm saw the pair of Sheriff Miller's deputies straighten up and step forward, faces grim.

"What are you going to do?" Bodie asked.

"I'm going to ask these men to pretend that they didn't see us."

"And if they won't do that?"

"I'm not sure," Longarm admitted. "I don't want to have to fight 'em."

"I'll help you," Bodie said. "I'm not afraid and I ain't goin' to let 'em arrest me and Homer."

"Let me see if they're going to be reasonable about this," Longarm told the boy.

Both of Sheriff Miller's deputies were big, strong young men, and Longarm knew they were going to insist on taking Bodie to jail.

"Marshal," the largest of the pair said, "we're

going to take this boy into custody. You weren't trying to take him out of town, were you?"

"As a matter of fact," Longarm admitted, "that's
exactly what I intend to do."

"Not a chance."

"The train is pulling out soon and we need to buy
Bodie a ticket."

"I guess you don't hear very well," the deputy said.
"I don't want any trouble with you . . . but that's your
choice. We have our orders and the kid is coming
with us."

"I have to take him to Virginia City."

The two big deputies exchanged glances, and a
message seemed to pass unspoken between them,
because they both reached for their guns.

Longarm saw the moves coming and drove a fist
into the bigger man's nose, breaking it with a sick-
ening crunching sound. The deputy staggered, and
Longarm slammed a hand down on the second deputy's forearm so hard that the man's Colt went flying.
Before he could recover, Longarm drove a vicious
left hook into his solar plexus and the deputy dropped
to his knees, gasping for breath, face contorted with
pain.

Longarm collected their pistols and said, "You
men mean well and I'm sorry that I had to hurt you,
but when you went for your guns, you gave me no
choice."

The larger one, whose nose had just been broken,
had his face cupped in his hands. Blood was dripping
through his fingers and he just shook his head.

"We're going to buy this boy a ticket, board the train with his dog, and be on our way. And you boys are going to watch us pull out of the station. If you do what I tell you, I'll toss your pistols out the window at the far end of the loading platform. If you don't do what I say, you'll have to go back to your office unarmed."

"What the hell are we going to tell Sheriff Miller!" the man on his knees cried.

"Tell him that some men jumped you from behind and you put up one hell of a hard fight."

"Clyde won't believe that!"

"Then think of something better," Longarm told the deputy. "It's not my problem. Bodie, let's get that ticket and board the train before all the good seats are taken."

Bodie was grinning. "You sure hit 'em fast and hard!"

"Sometimes there's no other way to keep a man from getting himself killed," Longarm said as they walked away.

As they were boarding, the conductor held up his hand and said, "You aren't planning on taking that dog on the train, are you?"

"I'm afraid we are," Longarm replied.

"I can't let you do that."

"You have no choice," Longarm said, showing the man his badge. "This is official business."

The conductor shrugged. "All right. But if it bites a passenger, it'll be your problem and not mine."

"Fair enough."

"And if it shits on the train, I'm not cleaning it up."

"We'll take care of that."

"Then welcome aboard!"

Ten minutes later Longarm waved good-bye to the pair of deputies and then pitched their guns out the window and watched the pistols bounce across the loading platform. He saw the pair hurry over and snatch up their weapons.

"You think they'll come after us?" Bodie asked.

"Nope. And I bet they'll come up with one hell of a good story to explain that broken nose," Longarm said.

"I sure would like to learn how to fight like you," Bodie told him.

"Well," Longarm replied, "you might just see a lot more fighting before this whole mess is over."

Bodie glanced sideways at Longarm and grinned.

Chapter 11

Longarm and Bodie settled into their seats, with Homer lying in the aisle and blocking it completely.

"That dog is going to have to move," the conductor said. "We've got to keep the aisles clear for people to pass through the coaches."

"Where is he supposed to be?" Bodie asked.

"In a cattle car."

Bodie shook his head. "Mister, the dog stays with me."

The conductor shook his head. "Tell you what, Marshal Long. The next coach up is almost empty. Why don't you three move up there and you'll have a whole bunch of seats to yourself, and that beast can rest wherever it chooses."

"Suits me," Longarm said.

"Me too," Bodie agreed.

And that's how they worked it all the way up to Cheyenne. Later, when they transferred to the Union

Pacific, they were happy to again find a nearly empty car, where they settled in for the night. They passed over the Laramie Mountains, and morning found them on the sagebrush-covered high plains of western Wyoming.

"When do they start serving breakfast?" Longarm asked as he gazed out at the familiar passing landscape.

"They've been serving for over an hour," the conductor answered. "But you can't take that dog into the dining car."

"Why not?" Bodie asked.

"Because it's against the rules and the dining staff would murder me if I let you bring a dog into their car."

"Couldn't we just tie Homer up beside the seat and bring him back some food and water?" Longarm asked.

"That would be fine."

Later that day Longarm turned to his young friend and asked, "You said you'd never been on a train before."

"That's right."

"Then how did you and John Stock get from Bodie to Denver?"

"We begged rides. Once, we paid and rode a stagecoach. Sometimes we just walked. It took over a month and wore us down. Getting over the Rocky Mountains was the hardest."

"Well, then, riding this train must seem like quite a luxury."

"It sure is," Bodie agreed. "This is the best time I've ever had just sitting here with you and Homer, watching the world pass by and not havin' to do a thing."

Longarm pointed out the window. "The next stop is going to be at Rock Springs to take on coal and water. Bodie, do you know anything about the history of this transcontinental railroad?"

"Just a little bit. I heard it was a race of some kind between the Central Pacific out of Sacramento and the Union Pacific coming from the east out of Omaha."

"That's right."

"And I heard that it was the Chinamen who pushed the Central Pacific over the Sierras. I knew a couple of Chinamen in Bodie, and they were good fellas. Kinda quiet and standoffish, but nice enough."

"They are good people. A lot of them that helped build the railroad over Donner Pass and then across Nevada went back to China with their money. I heard that they saved most of what they earned so they could help their families and buy farmland. But quite a few Chinese stayed in the mining camps, and there's a huge Chinatown in San Francisco."

"What about the men who built the railroad for the Union Pacific? What happened to all of them?"

"Some stayed out in the West, some went back east or to the South, where they were born and raised. A lot of the construction workers were ex–Civil War soldiers. Many were riffraff and were escaping the law or their creditors, but once on the job they all pulled together to lay track across the Great Plains.

Mostly, they had to worry about blizzards and Indians. But it was quite a race, and we're going to see where the railroads met at a place called Promontory Point in the Utah Territory."

Bodie grinned. "We gonna get to see that golden spike I heard was pounded into the joinin'?"

"No," Longarm said, "I'm sure that they pulled it up long ago or someone would have stolen it. But there's a statue and a little museum there that tells travelers the tale of the transcontinental race, and we'll hold over there for an hour or so tomorrow morning."

"I wish I could read better," Bodie said. "They probably have the whole story written out on signs, but I'm such a poor reader that most won't mean a thing to me."

"I'll read what you can't. Bodie, I know you've had it pretty rough all your young life, but I've got a hunch things are going to get much better for you in a hurry. And one thing you need to do is to get a little schooling so that you can read and do numbers."

"I can add and subtract," Bodie said proudly. "I got a knack for numbers and do 'em in my head all the time."

"That's good to hear," Longarm said.

When their train pulled into Rock Springs, everyone got off to walk around and get a little exercise. The conductor said that they'd have one hour to see the small town and then they'd need to reboard. Anyone not back from shopping or sightseeing would be left behind.

"Come on," Longarm told the kid. "There's not

much to see in Rock Springs, but we can get a bite
to eat and stretch our legs."

"Sure enough," Bodie said.

But the minute they disembarked, the town sheriff
spotted Longarm and hurried on over to greet him.
"Marshal Long, good to see you passin' through
again."

"Likewise."

Longarm introduced Bodie and his dog, then said,
"Were you looking for me?"

"I was," the sheriff answered, reaching into his
pocket and extracting a telegram. "I've got what I
figure is a pretty important message for you from
Marshal Vail in Denver."

The telegram was short and very disturbing.

MARSHAL CUSTIS LONG **STOP** MISS GLORIA
HARMON FOUND BEATEN TO DEATH IN HER
SHOP **STOP** MURDER MAY RELATE TO OTHER
BODIE RELATED KILLINGS **STOP** BE CAREFUL
ON TRAIN AND WHEN YOU GET TO RENO **STOP**

Longarm crushed the telegram in his clenched fist
and took a few steps off to be alone. He had never
imagined that anyone would harm, much less murder,
Gloria, and if she was beaten that could mean that
whoever killed her had been seeking information
about Bodie and perhaps even Longarm. But why!
Longarm's eyes burned with tears, and he roughly
scrubbed them away with his sleeve.

"I'm sorry," the sheriff said. "I take it from your
reaction that the woman meant a great deal to you."

"She did," Longarm said, clearing his throat and turning back to the lawman. "Miss Harmon was a fine young woman, and I will never rest until I find whoever murdered her and watch him hang."

"Are you getting on the eastbound and heading right back to Denver?"

"No," Longarm said, making a quick decision. "The murderer might be on this train posing as just another passenger. And even more, this trouble all comes from someone on the Comstock Lode and has to do with things that I have to figure out there."

"Well," the sheriff said, "I'm sorry for this bad news. Would you like me to send a telegram back to your boss?"

"Yeah," Longarm decided. "Tell Marshal Vail that I will be continuously on my guard while on this train and when we get to Reno."

"This all sounds pretty sinister and complicated."

"It is," Longarm said. "Bodie, let's take a walk around town."

"Yes, sir."

Once they were alone, Bodie asked, "Does that woman's dyin' have anything to do with me?"

"I can't possibly know that it does or not . . . but my guess is that Gloria's death has a great deal to do with you, your mother, and Mr. Burlington."

"Maybe I should buy a gun right here in Rock Springs," Bodie suggested.

Longarm nodded. "You ever shot a gun or rifle?"

"I've shot a rifle before. Killed a few rabbits for the pot. But never a pistol."

"In that case," Longarm said, "I think it's time

you learned how to shoot a revolver, and I know a very competent gunsmith here in Rock Springs. He will sell you a used Colt at a fair price."

"Can I shoot it a few times before we get back on the train?" Bodie asked with excitement.

"I think that would be a fine idea."

Bodie almost started running, but Longarm held him up and said, "I'm going to start teaching you how to shoot straight and handle a gun so you'll never accidentally shoot yourself."

"I sure would be grateful for the lessons."

Longarm put his mind on the gun that they'd buy for Bodie and tried not to dwell on the devastating news he'd just received from Denver. One way or another though, he was going to get to the bottom of this murderous mess, and when he did, blood was going to flow.

Chapter 12

Longarm bought Bodie a well-used but very service-able .44-40 Colt Single Action revolver and a couple of boxes of shells. Thirty minutes later, as the train whistle was blasting to tell everyone to get back on board, they stood about fifty yards from the tracks and practiced shooting at discarded beer bottles and tin cans.

"Bodie, the thing of it is," Longarm said, sending a rusty bean can jumping into the air and then drilling it a second time before it hit the ground, "you have to learn to point and fire without putting a lot of thought into the process."

"What about aiming?"

"You aim a rifle, you sort of learn to point a pistol," Longarm explained. "At least that's the way I was told to shoot. And you have to remember that most gunfights call for close and fast shooting. You have to be steady and fire accurately, but quick. Try to draw a gun faster than you're capable of doing and you'll either shoot yourself in the foot or miss."

"Fast, but not too fast."

"That's right," Longarm said, holstering his gun and then demonstrating.

"You're *really* fast!"

"There are faster men out there, and I've had the misfortune to face a few."

"Then how come, if they were faster, you're still alive?"

"Luck and nerves. I've been shot a few times, but if a man can keep his nerves steady, even wounded he can still shoot and kill his enemy. I've never met a man that could fire twice before I could get off my first bullet that kills him."

"I sure wouldn't like to get shot," Bodie said, reloading his six-gun.

"Nobody wants to die in a gunfight," Longarm said. "And if I even sense that someone is going to go for his gun and try to shoot me, I'll draw and shoot first."

"But what if the fella wasn't really going to go for his gun?"

Longarm shrugged. "To my way of thinking, you have to err on the side that will keep you alive."

"I'd say that was good advice," Bodie agreed. "You ever kill a man with a shotgun?"

"Yes."

"Did you blow his head plumb off?"

"Once I did," Longarm admitted. "Mostly, you try for the body. If a man gets hit with a shotgun blast, he won't be a danger to anyone ever again."

"Maybe I should have bought a shotgun instead," Bodie mused. "There were a couple of nice used ones in that man's shop, and they didn't cost much more than this pistol that I can't shoot straight."

"You can't walk around town carrying a shotgun," Longarm said.

"Why not?"

"Because it makes people really nervous."

"To hell with 'em! I don't care if they get nervous or not."

"Listen, Bodie, I bought you a holster, and that's where you keep your pistol. And you don't fool with it around strangers, because that makes them very edgy. If you're in a saloon, and you reach for your gun, someone is liable to go for his own weapon and you'll be dead."

"I could hit *anything* with a shotgun."

"But you'd have no range, and there are a lot of places that won't allow a man to bring a shotgun inside."

"Okay," Bodie said, "then I'll just have to learn to shoot fast and straight with this Colt."

"That would be my advice."

Bodie fired at a nearby can three times, hitting it once but missing it twice. "You think there is anything *wrong* with this pistol?" he asked.

"Like what for instance?" Longarm glanced over his shoulder at the train and saw the conductor waving for them to hurry over and get on board. "We're running short of time."

"Trains start off real slow," Bodie said, firing his pistol and missing. "Maybe the fella that owned this gun before me sold it to your gunsmith friend because the barrel was bent."

Longarm almost laughed out loud. "Bodie, there is nothing wrong with that pistol. It's had plenty of use, but it's a fine weapon. You're just a poor shot. It takes a lot of practice and that means buying plenty of ammunition."

"But I don't have time to practice before we get to Virginia City."

"No," Longarm admitted, "you don't. But we bought a couple boxes of shells, and every time our train stops for water and coal, we'll step off and take a few practice rounds. Now, come on and let's get back on board. Where's your wolf dog?"

"Hell if I know. Could I shoot *your* gun?"

"No," Longarm said. "A man's gun is like a man's woman. You just don't lend it out to anyone."

Bodie fired once more and this time kicked up enough dirt to move the can. "I'm getting closer," he said.

The train gave off one last shrill whistle, but Bodie either didn't notice or care as his eyes searched for his dog. "Homer!" he yelled. "Come along, Homer!"

Homer struggled out from behind a broken-down wagon, dragging a female dog as he tried hard to disengage himself.

"Damn!" Bodie cried as the train started to move. "He's swelled up in her and is stuck!"

"We have to leave him and catch that train," Longarm shouted as it began to roll.

"But I can't leave Homer like that!"

"Dammit, Bodie," Longarm yelled over his

shoulder, "I'm not waiting around while your dog tries to uncouple!"

"He'll be loose of her in just a minute or two."

"And by then the train will have left us here in Rock Springs!" Longarm shouted, breaking into a run and hauling himself up onto the caboose. "Come on, Bodie!"

The kid ran over to his huge dog and gave him a hard kick up between its legs. Homer howled in pain and broke free, and then the pair was racing after the train. Longarm didn't think they'd make it, but somehow they both jumped up on the caboose and collapsed, gasping for air.

"You're a hell of a fast runner," Longarm said to the boy. "And that dog of yours . . . well, I just think maybe from now on you'd better lead him on a rope when we stop or he's going to either get left or get shot."

"Yeah," Bodie said, finally regaining his breath, "I guess that'd be a good idea. But he sure likes to ride those stray bitches."

"It's a common failing," Longarm said, feeling his cheeks warm as the train left Rock Springs farther and farther behind.

Chapter 13

Longarm and Bodie used up all their practice ammunition during the rest of their trip, and when they boarded the train out of Lovelock, Nevada, they settled in for the last leg of their trip with no plans for further practice.

Several hours later, they were rolling into Reno.

"Next stop, Reno!" the conductor called out and he moved from coach to coach. When he came abreast of Longarm and Bodie, he said, "Can't say I'm sorry to say good-bye to that big dog. Are you bringing him back to Cheyenne on this train?"

"Don't know yet," Bodie answered.

"I'm going to have to have someone really clean and scrub this passenger car because that mongrel shit and pissed in it, and my boss is going to be especially furious that your damned dog completely chewed the arm off that seat."

"Sorry about that," Longarm offered. "But we all

have to deal with the unexpected. I think you, your boss, and the Union Pacific will survive the trouble and loss."

"Sure, easy for you to say, Marshal. Still and all, I'd be obliged if you could let me know if the boy and his dog are returning with you, so that I can make sure that I'm on a different run."

Longarm shook his head. "Conductor, I've got a murder to investigate, and it might involve this boy's mother. So do you really think I'm going to be thinking about your petty inconvenience?"

The conductor paused and then said, "No, and I really hope that the boy's mother is safe."

"Thanks," Bodie said as the train rolled to a stop.

"Well, now the work begins," Longarm said. "Are you sure you want to go up to Virginia City?"

"I sure do."

"I've got a little matter to take care of before we leave town, but I think I'll have it wrapped up in a day."

"Does that mean we have to stay here a day?"

"I'm afraid that it does."

Bodie couldn't hide his disappointment. "Maybe I could get some ammunition tomorrow morning and do some more practicing."

"That would be a good idea. I'll go with you and then go visit the town sheriff. You and Homer can just take it easy and see the sights tomorrow."

"I'm getting a lot better with the Colt, aren't I?"

"Of course you are! Bodie, you're already more than a decent shot with that pistol we picked up in Rock Springs."

"I sure can't shoot anywhere near as good as you."

"Not yet, you can't. But I think you've gotten to know the gun and feel comfortable handling and firing it. That was our main goal to get done before we hit this town."

"Maybe I'll have to use it if someone murdered my mother. I'd kill 'em in the blink of an eye, Marshal. I'd do it even if it meant getting hanged."

"You don't owe your mother your life, kid, and I don't think she'd want you to swing from a noose on her account. Anyway, why don't you leave that kind of business to me," Longarm cautioned. "I'm a federal marshal, and if I have to kill a man, I've got some legal protections. But if *you* killed someone . . . even if that somebody was responsible for the death of your mother . . . it would go hard, and the best you could hope for would be prison."

"I killed that man in Denver and they didn't do anything to me."

"Yes, you did," Longarm said. "But I was witness to that shooting and a part of it too, so you were in the clear. What we have now is a whole different thing."

"Murder is murder."

"That's right, Bodie, and after learning about the tragic death of my friend Gloria, I've been thinking that John Stock wasn't the real target that day we first met on Colfax Avenue."

Bodie was quiet for a moment before he asked, "Do you think they really wanted to kill *me*?"

"Either that or capture you and make you sign a document saying you have no rights to any property that might have been left by either your mother or her husband."

Bodie nodded with understanding. "You're expecting someone to try to kill me again, aren't you."

It wasn't a question.

"I'm afraid that is a real possibility," Longarm admitted. "And that's why I thought it was so important to buy you a reliable pistol and that you have a little time to practice shooting it."

"If someone wanted to kill me, they'd have to kill Homer first."

"Homer wouldn't even know who fired the bullet," Longarm said, his tone grave. "I'm not saying that your dog isn't going to be helpful if we're attacked. I'm just telling you that neither I nor Homer can stop a well-aimed ambusher's bullet."

"I understand."

Longarm pulled out his watch and noted the time. "It's four. We'll get a hotel room, have a nice dinner, and then get a good night's sleep. Tomorrow I'll take care of whatever business I'm supposed to do so that I can be here officially. I'll also get us paid up for a ride to Virginia City the following morning."

"I could use sleeping in a bed," Bodie admitted. "I like traveling on a train, but it's hard sleeping in a seat night after night."

"I know." Longarm reached for his bag. "When we get off the train, keep your eyes open for trouble."

Bodie's eyebrows rose in question. "Do you think that someone *knows* we're coming into this town today and might try and kill us?"

"It's entirely possible."

"But how would they know?"

"Same way I learned about the death of my friend. A telegraph is a whole lot faster than a train."

"So what do we do when we get off?"

"Just watch everyone on the loading platform. If you see a man watching only us, or reaching into his coat pocket, or maybe coming right at us, then give me a loud warning shout."

"What if there is *more* than one man?"

Longarm stood up and started down the aisle. "In that case you had better remember how to shoot straight and fast, because that's what I'll be doing."

"I'll remember," Bodie promised as he untied Homer and followed Longarm off the car.

Chapter 14

Longarm and Bodie stepped off the train and into the jam of passengers that were disembarking at Reno. They stood and studied everyone in sight, but no one stood out as an obvious and immediate threat. After a few minutes, Longarm started moving. He knew that any ambusher might well be hiding outside the train station, and when they were clear of it, Longarm took a long, careful look around.

"See anyone that looks like trouble?" Bodie asked, shifting his bag and keeping a tight hold on Homer.

"No. Let's head for a hotel I like up near the Truckee River Bridge."

It wasn't a very long walk, and once again Longarm was struck by how easy Reno was on the eye. Unlike the Nevada rail towns of Elko, Battle Mountain, and Winnemucca, Reno had a look of permanence and beauty. The downtown buildings were mostly constructed of red brick instead of the cheaper and fire-prone rough wooden planks so typical in Western towns. And there were trees and sidewalks, all giving Reno an air of unmistakable permanency. But the very nicest and most picturesque part of the town was the clear, cold, and sparkling Truckee River flowing year-round right through the center of Reno.

"It's almost as handsome as Denver, I'd say," Bodie offered. "But a lot smaller."

"It'll grow," Longarm told the kid. "The Comstock Lode riches have helped Reno to prosper, but the railroad, ranching, and logging all add their share to the prosperity."

"I wouldn't mind living here. Sure is a lot prettier than Bodie."

Longarm almost chuckled, because almost anywhere was prettier than the rough, raw Bodie. "Here we are."

"Nice hotel. Are they going to let Homer in?"

"I hope so. If not, we'll just have to find another hotel, and there are plenty to choose from."

The hotel desk clerk was a short, heavyset man in his thirties with wire-rimmed spectacles that were perched on a hooked nose. "Well Marshal Long! It's been a while since we had the pleasure of your company."

"Thanks, Arthur. I need a room and my friend and his dog need a second room of their own. Can you help us?"

Arthur stared at the wolf dog. "I'm afraid that the owners won't allow a dog in our rooms."

"Well then," Longarm said, "I guess we'll have to find some place else."

"I'm very sorry," Arthur said with regret. "But I have to follow the rules or I'll lose my job."

"I don't want that to happen. Do you have any suggestions where else we can stay a couple of nights?"

"The Mapes Hotel might take you. They have downstairs rooms with private entrances and little enclosed patios."

"That would work. Thanks, Arthur."

The Mapes Hotel was just a block away and right beside the river. Longarm and Bodie had no trouble booking adjoining rooms and the price was reasonable. "We have a fine restaurant that serves breakfast, lunch, and dinner," the desk clerk informed them.

"We'll keep that in mind," Longarm promised.

After they'd settled in their rooms, Longarm felt like taking a nap, but it was early in the afternoon, so he freshened up and then told Bodie, "I'm going to pay a visit to the local sheriff's office. I'll be back in an hour or two and we can go get something to eat. You should stay here in your room and keep the door to the hallway as well as the one to the patio locked until I return."

"What happens when me or Homer needs to take a leak or crap?"

"Well, in that case, sure. But carry your gun and watch out for trouble."

Fifteen minutes later Longarm strode into Sheriff Newt Bolden's office and caught the man snoozing with his feet up on his desk.

"Another rough day maintaining law and order in

Reno, huh?" Longarm asked, giving the man a nudge and waking him with a start.

"Why if it isn't Marshal Custis Long! How are you doin'?"

"I'm fine."

"Like a cup of strong, cold coffee?"

Over the years Newt's cold coffee had almost become a standing joke between them. "How could I resist such an offer?"

"I'll pour us both a cup. I suppose you're here about the murder of United States Marshal Hugh Parker."

"To tell you the truth, there are so many things going on that my boss, Marshal Vail, didn't even give me the deceased's name."

"Huh!" Bolden shook his head. "Marshal Parker's gun and money were missing, and when he was found behind a saloon, he was unconscious. We hoped he'd wake up and be able to tell us something, but he passed away early this morning."

Longarm took a sip of the sheriff's coffee and tried not to grimace. "Good as always, Newt."

"Yeah, I do like it strong." Newt plopped down in his chair and threw his boots back up on his desk. "Did you know Federal Officer Hugh Parker?"

"No. We had never met."

"No, him being from the San Francisco office and you being from Denver, I don't suppose you would have met."

"What was he like?" Longarm asked.

"Marshal Parker was hard to read. He kept his own counsel and didn't tell me much, but I knew he was investigating that murder up in Virginia City."

"What murder?"

"The one where a wealthy couple was murdered and burned up in their mansion."

Longarm almost dropped his cup. "And their names?"

"Chester and Ruby Burlington. I met them a few times when they came down here to shop or just to get away from the Comstock Lode to see a river and trees again. They were as nice a couple as you'd ever meet and it was clear they were very much in love."

"Did they arrest those responsible?"

"Afraid not." Newt shook his head. "At first, everyone thought that Mr. and Mrs. Burlington had died accidentally. Chester Burlington always had a lit cigar in his mouth."

"But their deaths weren't an accident?"

"Their bodies were charred almost beyond recognition, but the mortician found a bullet hole in the back of each of their skulls."

Longarm leaned forward with intense interest. "In the back, not the side or front?"

"No, in the back of the head. Dead center. Small-caliber bullets but obviously lethal. So it was pretty obvious they'd been murdered, and because their safe door was hanging open it didn't seem a stretch to figure out that they had been forced to open the safe and then were murdered, and their home was burned down around their bodies to hide the cause of their deaths."

"Yes, whoever killed them probably thought that the bodies would be too charred for anyone to note the bullet holes," Longarm mused aloud.

"That's the way that I saw it, and so did Marshal Hugh Parker. Of course, I couldn't go up to Virginia City even to see the crime scene because it's out of my jurisdiction."

"What about the local Virginia City authorities?"

"The only man they had is gone. The Comstock Lode's production has fallen off so much that the town has almost no revenue and is dead broke. They had to lay off their entire city staff and that included the only lawman on their payroll."

"That usually happens when the gold peters out," Longarm said. "And when everybody starts closing their business and striking out for the newer mining discoveries."

"Yeah. There are still about a thousand people living in Virginia City hoping that some new pocket of gold or silver will be found, but most people think that the town is in for a slow death."

"I'd agree that is likely."

"Custis, you can buy mines and claims up there for a penny on the dollar now. Houses and businesses are going for next to nothing."

"Kind of hate to see that," Longarm said. "In her day, Virginia City was a sight to behold. I've never been in any boomtown where the liquor and the money flowed as fast and free."

"Oh, it was wild and wicked, all right," Newt agreed with a smile. "The life expectancy of a sheriff up there was about a month."

"So tell me what United States Marshal Hugh Parker found out while investigating the Burlington murder and arson?"

"He was on to something, but he never quite got around telling me exactly what it was."

"You mean," Longarm asked, "that he thought he knew who might have murdered and then burned that couple to death?"

"I think he had his suspicions and was trying to round up some solid evidence."

"Well he must have told you *something*."

"Custis, Hugh Parker was real closemouthed. He would have told me when he thought the time was right, but someone got to him before that time."

"Tell me everything you known about Hugh Parker and how he died."

"Not much to tell. Marshal Parker was in his thirties, a good-lookin' fella who had an eye for women and a thirst for drink. When he was staying here in Reno, he was seeing a young woman named Katie Lund."

"Is she a prostitute?"

"No. She does bookwork for a lawyer here in Reno named Jake Kelsey. I met Katie a few times and liked her, but I sure never liked her lawyer boss."

"Why didn't you like Jake Kelsey?"

"Because," Newt said, "he's as crooked as a sidewinder and as cunning as a coyote."

"What else can you tell me about Marshal Hugh Parker?"

"Not much. He was sent off by the feds from San Francisco, and he wasn't here but two weeks. He didn't like staying up in Virginia City, and I had the feeling that he felt . . . well, threatened up there on the Comstock Lode."

"Threatened by whom?" Longarm asked.

"I'm not sure. But when the news got out that Mr. and Mrs. Chester Burlington had been shot in the back of their heads, everything changed, and you could just feel the anger and tension in Marshal Hugh Parker. He'd come over from San Francisco thinking he was looking at an accident and maybe a robbery and then suddenly he was investigating a cold-blooded murder."

"Did he have any leads as to who might have done it?"

"Like I said, Marshal Parker was pretty close-mouthed, and he played his hand close to the vest. I knew that he'd eventually tell me what he knew and not a minute earlier, so I didn't press him. After all, the murder up there wasn't in my jurisdiction."

"Yeah, you said that."

"Well," Sheriff Bolden said a little defensively, "that's the truth of it."

"I know." Longarm forced himself to take a sip of a coffee so strong it would have corroded a horseshoe. "But maybe he told his gal, Katie Lund, a few things I ought to know. Even a good lawman will say things in bed with a woman that he wouldn't tell anyone else."

"Is that a fact?" Newt asked.

"You know that it is," Longarm said, seeing a smile tugging at the corners of the man's mouth. "So I think I'd better go and have a talk with Katie Lund. Where is her attorney's office?"

"Just up the street a block. You can't miss it. Big red-brick two-story building with a white wooden balcony off the second floor overlooking Virginia Street. Attorney Kelsey likes to sit up over the sidewalk and wave at people he thinks might have money enough to pay him to solve their legal problems."

"He sounds like a real hustler to me," Longarm said.

"Oh, he is." The sheriff glanced over at an old grandfather clock. "If you want some advice, I'd tell you to wait about an hour, till Attorney Kelsey heads out his door, and then go up and talk to Miss Lund."

"And why would I have to wait?"

"Just a suggestion," Newt Bolden said, raising his hands palms up. "No use in causing a stir when it can be helped."

"I'll take your suggestion," Longarm said, sensing that the man was just giving him a friendly warning not to get involved with the attorney.

"We can sit here and chew the fat for an hour," Newt suggested. "You can tell me about all the dangerous and deadly criminals you've shot since last we got together, but I'd rather hear about all the women you've screwed."

"You're a dirty and lecherous old fart," Longarm said with a laugh.

"You pegged me just right. You about ready for another cup of coffee?"

"Nope."

"Better drink 'er down before she's gone."

"I'll take my chances, Newt."

"Suit yourself," Reno's congenial town sheriff said, as he got up to pour himself another cold cup.

Chapter 15

Longarm visited with Sheriff Bolden until five o'clock, and then he walked up the street and stood opposite the lawyer's office. Bolden had described Katie Lund as being a very attractive woman about five feet, two inches tall, with long, dark brown hair, a nice figure, and a "perky" walk, whatever that meant.

At about a quarter after five, Longarm saw a woman who fit that description exit the brick building where Jake Kelsey practiced law. She turned and walked south moving at a brisk pace.

"Gotta be her," Longarm said to himself as he crossed the street and hurried to overtake the woman. When he did, he said, "Excuse me, are you Miss Katie Lund?"

She turned and looked up at him. "What if I am?"

Longarm removed his badge and flashed it before

her face. "I'd like a few minutes of your time, Miss Lund."

"What is this about?" she asked, not stopping.

"It's about a boy named Bodie, who I think lost his mother and stepfather up in Virginia City. Mr. and Mrs. Burlington? And also the death of Marshal Hugh Parker."

Katie stopped and turned to gaze up into his face. "I don't recognize you."

"I'm sorry, I didn't introduce myself. My name is Custis Long, and I'm a deputy United States marshal who works out of the Denver office. I'm here on official business concerning the murder of the boy's mother. Reno's Sheriff Newt Bolden said that you knew Marshal Parker."

"I won't deny it."

"Could we please go somewhere and talk?"

Katie frowned. "I'm not sure that I can tell you anything that would help you solve Hugh's murder."

"You might be wrong about that, and it wouldn't take long to find out. Ten, fifteen minutes, Miss Lund. I've come a long way to work on this case and I need your help."

She thought about it for a second or two and then nodded her head. "There's a little place up the street called Clancy's Bar and Steak House, where I like to stop and have a drink and sometimes a meal before going home. If you buy me a shot or two of good Irish whiskey and a corned beef and rye sandwich, I'll tell you what I can about Hugh and the Burlington murder."

"It's a deal."

*   *   *

Ten minutes later they were seated at a small, dark table in a fine Irish drinking and eating establishment that was already starting to fill up with the evening's customers.

"I'll have my usual glass of Brannigan's Best," Katie told the smiling waiter, who sported a handlebar mustache the equal of Longarm's. "And a corned beef on rye sandwich."

"Very good," the man said with a thick Irish brogue. "And the gentleman?"

"The same."

The waiter disappeared but returned in a few minutes with two brandy snifters filled with a richly colored whiskey. "Do you want to eat soon?" he asked.

"Maybe a half hour," Katie told him. "Thanks, Clancy."

"My pleasure, dear girl." The owner of the establishment smiled at Longarm. "New to Reno, are we?"

"Yes."

"I hope you'll enjoy your stay. You certainly have found excellent company!"

"Clancy is old enough to be my father," Katie said, but he'd like to be my boyfriend."

"He's not married?"

"I don't know. If he is, I've never heard him speak of his wife or any children. Clancy is from Dublin, and he came to the Comstock Lode about ten years ago and opened a saloon up on C Street that made him a small fortune. He sold that saloon about three years ago when he saw the writing on the wall and knew that the ore was starting to peter out. He's done very well here in Reno, but he has a wicked mind and a roving eye."

Longarm raised his glass in toast. The Irish whiskey went down smoothly, and it warmed its way clear down to his stomach. "Excellent," he proclaimed.

"Yes, isn't it? Now," Katie said, "what do you want to know?"

"As I said, I have Mrs. Burlington's son with me. Bodie is fourteen, and it now seems that he is also an orphan. He has had a very difficult childhood and was involved in some trouble in Denver. I helped him out, and we found a letter from his mother that was bloodstained, saying she had married Mr. Burlington, found religion, and wanted him to come live with her and her new husband."

"But then you found out that they were murdered up in Virginia City."

"That's right," Longarm said. "And I also need to find out who murdered Marshal Parker and left him to die behind a saloon."

"It was *this* saloon."

Longarm blinked. "Marshal Parker died in the alley behind this saloon?"

"That's right. Didn't our sheriff mention that?"

"No. He must have thought it was unimportant."

"Maybe it was," Katie said. "Hugh and I used to come here after work, just like we're doing today. We'd have a few drinks and a sandwich or some Irish stew and soda bread. Sometimes corned beef and cabbage. We liked this atmosphere and we liked the whiskey and good food."

"Easy to see why you liked the whiskey. So what happened on the night Hugh Parker was murdered?"

Katie shrugged. "We had more to drink than normal that evening and the hour grew late. Hugh was pretty drunk and talking loudly. Clancy even had to come over a couple of times and ask him to quiet down a little."

"Was he talking about the Burlington murders?"

"Yes. He was excited because he said he had found some evidence that might really prove who the killer or killers were."

"And people overheard this?"

Katie nodded and emptied her glass, signaling for a refill. "Hugh said that there was a connection between the murder and a legal issue that was being introduced to our court in a few days."

"What kind of 'legal issue' was he talking about?"

"The last will and testimony of Chester and Ruby Burlington."

"I see." Longarm thought a moment. "Why wouldn't the Story County court hear that issue?"

"Because that court has been shut down, so now all legal matters from Story County are sent down here to Washoe County."

"Now I understand. Katie, I have to ask you a question that is very important—was your boss, Jake Kelsey, involved in this court case?"

"As of today he is." Katie accepted her refill and took a deep swallow. "I didn't know that it was going to turn out like this. Hugh and I were friends, and a little more. When he was murdered, I just figured that he got into a fight with someone here after I left and it turned out to be the cause of his death."

"And what do you believe now?"

She shook her head. "I believe that you believe that Hugh's death and the death of the Burlington couple are somehow intertwined." She stared into his eyes. "Am I right?"

"Yes," Longarm said, "you are. Did Hugh Parker say anything that would help me find out who murdered the Burlington couple? I have to find some answers for Ruby Burlington's son, and he might just be entitled to a sizable inheritance."

"Do you think so?"

"Why not? Did Hugh Parker ever tell you if Mr. Burlington had any heirs?"

"One. Apparently, he has a son that lives in Virginia City who is a gambler and owner of a mine on the verge of being closed down. Hugh said he had met the son a few times and that there was bad blood between him and his wealthy father."

"I see."

Longarm glanced away, his mind whirling with possibilities. It made sense that the son might be the person who either murdered the Burlingtons or paid to have someone else do the job.

"What's the boy like?" Katie asked quietly.

"Bodie is a good boy, but very rough around the edges. He had to kill a man in Denver."

"Kill him!"

"Please," Longarm said, "could you hold your voice down a little?"

"I'm sorry. But what a shock. You show up with

a boy whose mother was murdered and burned to char, and in the next breath you tell me that this fourteen-year-old boy had to kill a man? That's pretty shocking, Marshal Long."

"Call me Custis. And yes, you're right. It is shocking."

"So what are you doing with the boy?"

"He's at a hotel close by. I wanted to get a jump on this case today, and then in the morning we'll take a stagecoach up to Virginia City, where I was going to try to find out what I could about the murder of his mother."

"I met the Burlingtons," Katie said quietly. "Does the boy know the history of his mother?"

"Yes. But the last letter that she wrote, the one with bloodstains, was filled with happiness. She had found religion and a good husband. If the letter is to be believed, Ruby had changed and her new husband had completely forgiven her sordid past."

"Does the boy forgive his mother's past?"

"I honestly don't know. What I am sure of is that he will want to visit her grave, and he wants me to find out and bring to justice the one who killed his mother."

Katie drank and signaled a different waiter to bring another refill and their sandwiches. When the food came, they talked about Hugh Parker, and Longarm had the distinct impression that Katie had dumped the marshal the very night he was murdered.

"Hugh was handsome and fun, but he was a rogue and he was always flirting with other young women. Even when we were together. I could see that he was not the kind of man that I should ever fall in love with."

"That's pretty much in line with what Sheriff Bolden said about Hugh Parker."

"I'd like to meet the boy if you spend any time in Reno."

"Why?" Longarm asked bluntly.

"Because when I was a teenager I had a miscarriage and lost a son." Katie's words were a little slurred and sad. "And so I have a huge hole in my heart for boys, especially ones who didn't really have a decent mother."

"Bodie is hard," Longarm warned. "I think the only thing he cares about is his huge dog, Homer."

"He brought a dog all the way from Denver?"

"Yeah," Longarm said between bites of sandwich. "I could tell you a lot of stories about our trip out here on the train."

"I didn't even know you could take a dog on a train."

"If you're a federal marshal you can sometimes get things arranged that ordinarily wouldn't happen."

"Could I meet Bodie after we leave here?"

"Sure. But, Katie, you have to come at him real easy or he'll turn away. He doesn't trust anyone."

"Not even you?"

"Probably not even me," Longarm confessed.

Katie reached across the table and laid a hand on his forearm, then squeezed it. "Custis, let's have another round because you're buying, and then let's go see the boy and his dog. I like dogs almost as well as boys."

"That might change when you lay eyes on Homer. He's a wolf dog and he's not real friendly."

"Dogs and cats take to me right off," Katie promised. "They understand when a person is good or bad. That's another reason why I was getting rid of Hugh—he hated animals, and the feeling was mutual. Do you like dogs?"

"Yeah. Yeah I do."

"That's important," Katie said. "Very important."

Longarm was lost as to what that meant, but he had a feeling that Katie Lund had never gotten over the loss of her unborn child, and that she was a good person who probably led her life with her heart instead of her head. Much more importantly, she might remember a thing or two that Hugh Parker had told her the last time they'd been drinking Irish whiskey together here in this saloon.

Something that would bring this murder mystery full circle.

Chapter 16

Longarm asked Clancy to make up a sandwich and some fried and deliciously seasoned potato slices for Bodie, along with any meat scraps he had for Homer, while they had one more generous shot of Brannigan's Best.

By the time they arrived back at the Mapes Hotel, it was almost eleven o'clock and Longarm was feeling anxious about having left the boy and his dog alone so late. But he needn't have worried, because both were asleep and their door was locked.

"Bodie," Longarm said, "this is Miss Katie Lund. She knew your mother and stepfather and is going to help me find out what happened to them up in Virginia City."

Bodie rubbed his eyes, glanced at Custis, and said, "I thought we were going to have something to eat."

"I brought you and Homer a sack of food. I think you'll like what you find."

"Thanks," Bodie said without much enthusiasm. "Can we go up to Virginia City tomorrow?"

"Yes."

"Good. Hey, miss, don't get close to that dog!"

But Katie was already kneeling down and petting the huge animal. To everyone's surprise, Homer seemed to be enjoying the woman's attention, and when she reached into the bag and started feeding him scraps of fat and corned beef, Homer slobbered all over her hand and his big tail began to thump the floor.

"Well I'll be jingoes!" Bodie said. "I've never seen him take to a stranger like that before."

"Dogs like me because I like them. All of them. Big and small. Fierce and friendly. I own two dogs and three cats."

"You do?" Bodie was chewing furiously on his sandwich. "Big dogs or little?"

"Both, although my biggest dog isn't nearly as big as your Homer."

"Homer doesn't like other dogs, and he'll kill cats."

"Then I'll never have him over to my house," Katie said. "But I have a pen where he could stay while I make you and Custis a home-cooked steak some evening when you return from Virginia City."

"Or I could just tie him to a tree or something strong," Bodie offered. "He doesn't mind being tied up as long as I'm around."

"That would be fine too," Katie said. "Custis tells me that you lived most of your life in Bodie. I've never been there. Is it nice?"

"It's okay. Bad water. Lots of dust and wind. I like Reno and Denver a lot better. In Bodie there were no trees, because even the foul-tasting water had to be hauled a long way to the town."

"I see."

Longarm sat back, and for the next half hour, he just enjoyed listening to the pair talk about small things. He appreciated the fact that Katie didn't mention Ruby or her death or any other sad things that might upset Bodie. And all the time, Homer laid his massive head on Katie's lap and gazed fondly up into her kind brown but slightly bloodshot eyes.

Longarm hadn't expected Katie to accompany him next door to his hotel room, or to boldly step inside and begin to kiss his lips. He hadn't expected her body to be so luscious, either. But when they climbed into bed still slightly drunk and belching vapors of corned beef, he thought that he had just become the luckiest man in Reno.

Longarm made slow, passionate love to Katie, and their session ended with her on top, back arched, hair swinging from side to side as she laughed and then groaned with pleasure. When she finally reached orgasm, he rolled her over onto her hands and knees and entered her from behind. He thrust until his big hands stiffened on her narrow hips and he growled and gasped with release.

"I take it that was as good for you as it was for me," Katie said a few minutes later, while they were lying on their backs regaining their breath.

"Oh yeah," Longarm assured her. "It was."

Katie turned on her side and studied his face. "Custis?"

"Huh?"

"Hugh was a hard, dangerous man, but they killed him all the same. Please be very careful up in Virginia City and down here in Reno. Whoever killed Hugh might already know that you and the boy are here and determined to get to the bottom of the murders. If that's true, they'll make every effort to kill you and also Bodie."

"I know."

She kissed his face. "So, do you like Reno as well as Denver?"

"Reno is a very picturesque and enjoyable town."

"Do you think you might like to stay here for a while?"

He turned to look into her eyes. "Katie, I'm not the man for you. Please don't start thinking about things that aren't going to happen."

"Okay."

He kissed her, and then they lay back on their pillows and went to sleep.

Chapter 17

"Well, here we are," Longarm said, stepping down from the stagecoach in Virginia City. "Twenty years ago this place was a magnet for every starry-eyed dreamer and gold-fevered prospector in the world."

Bodie climbed out of the stagecoach. His dog had not been allowed inside, so Homer had trotted after the coach all the way from Reno. He still looked fresh, and because the weather was cool, Homer hadn't suffered.

"The cemetery is out there," Longarm said, pointing to the east. "Would you like to see if we can find your mother's grave?"

Bodie just nodded his head.

"All right, let's stretch our legs, and I'm sure that it won't be hard to find the gravesites of your mother and her husband."

Longarm's prediction proved correct. In less than thirty minutes, they were standing in front of two impressive headstones and what were clearly recently dug graves. There were even some wilted flowers strewn across Ruby's raised mound of dirt.

"I'll just wander around for a few minutes, and when you're done here, let out a shout and we'll go back into town and get rooms."

"Yes, sir."

Longarm had always had a bit of a fascination for graveyards. He wasn't morbid about them, but he liked reading the epitaphs, always hoping he could get a little insight into the person who was lying still and cold almost under his feet. As he wandered around the cemetery, he saw that the graves dated back to 1860, which was right around the time that the Comstock Lode ore had first been discovered. The town itself had been named after James "Old Virginny" Fennimore, and the story was that in 1859 "Old Virginny" had gotten roaring drunk and ridden up Gold Canyon only to topple off his horse and smash his last bottle of whiskey. Staggering to his feet, he had the great presence of mind to brush himself off, survey the dark stain of his bad whiskey, and shout to his equally drunken companions, "There dammit, I have just christened this place in my own gall-darned honor as Virginia City!"

Longarm didn't know if that was a true story or not, but he sure thought it was a good one.

"I'm ready now," Bodie said, joining him. "There are a lot of graves here."

"Yes. And most of them belong to Welsh hard-rock miners, and the main cause of their death was pneumonia."

"Why is that?"

"I'm far from an expert on deep, hard-rock mining, but I do know that some of these mines went a thousand feet deep. And that far down the temperature is very hot . . . maybe as hot as one hundred and fifty degrees. I'm told that the miner's union made sure that its members were paid three dollars a day and received a hundred pounds of ice per shift in those deepest and hottest levels."

"It must have been like working down in hell," Bodie opined.

"I think it was," Longarm agreed. "But three dollars a day was double what a cowboy would make and more than I make today as a federal marshal, so there were always men willing to risk their lives. But when they were brought up in cages dangling from cables, they were often overheated, and when they were hit by icy winter blasts, it was almost a certainty that they would catch pneumonia, and that's why so many died young up here on the Comstock Lode, so far away from their families."

Bodie nodded with understanding. "They have plenty of gold mines in Bodie, but none that go more than a hundred feet underground. I vowed I'd never work down in a deep mine. I'd rather shovel horseshit than risk being buried alive."

"I agree," Longarm said. "I remember reading that Dan DeQuille, a famous reporter who worked here on the *Territorial Enterprise*, said that if all the Comstock Lode mines were linked up in a straight line, they would stretch from here to San Francisco."

Bodie blinked with surprise. "Do you really believe that?"

"I do. Hard-rock miners been digging underneath our feet for over twenty-five years, and the earth below is now riddled with caverns and tunnels. I was told once that some of the bigger mines, like the Ophir, were so extensive that a person could get lost and wander around for weeks."

"My mother has a real nice headstone and so does her husband. Side by side. I'm glad I got to visit this cemetery, but I never want to return."

"That's perfectly understandable," Longarm assured the boy. "Now, let's go find a room and get something to eat."

As they walked back into town, Bodie asked, "How are you going to start findin' out who murdered my ma and her husband?"

"I'm going to do what I always do," Longarm replied. "I'll go by the newspaper office and read their past issues on the deaths. I'll also belly-up at bars and casually ask questions. The thing of it is, Bodie, most people fear death but they hold a fascination for it and want to talk endlessly about it. I'll go from one place and person to another and I'll find out plenty."

"I'd like to see where their mansion stood, even if it is just a pile of ashes."

"All right. We can visit it tomorrow."

"I'd rather visit it right away."

"Okay, just as soon as we get rooms and something to eat. I'm so hungry I could eat a sow and nine piglets and then chase their boar a half mile."

"Ha!" Bodie cried. "That's pretty danged hungry all right."

They had no trouble finding rooms cheap, because business was so poor; the dinner they ate didn't cost very much either, considering its quantity and quality.

When they walked out of the restaurant, Longarm said, "Bodie, that meal for both of us cost only seventy-five cents. When Virginia City was booming, a meal like that would have cost two dollars or more."

"Two dollars?"

"That's right. Everything costs more than it should in a boomtown. But now that its bust, the prices have gotten cheap."

"Let's go find the burned down mansion," Bodie said.

They found the ruins of the Burlington Mansion at the very end of A Street, overlooking miles of sagebrush-covered hills and valleys. The only things left standing were two opposing brick chimneys that marked where the master bedroom had stood, at the opposite end of the home from the living room, and a collapsed and heat-twisted iron staircase now leading to nowhere. There was evidence that some effort had been made by the local volunteer fire department to save the mansion, but the fire must have spread so quickly and with such intensity that their work had been futile.

"It was a huge house," Longarm said, as they stood by a stone staircase leading into the rubble. "A showpiece of a home."

"I wish I'd have been able to go inside it when my ma lived here and seen how fine it was."

"Yeah," Longarm said, "she must have been very proud of her new status in life."

Bodie walked right into the charred rubble. "I wonder if I can find anything important or valuable in all of this."

"I doubt it," Longarm told the boy. "There have probably already been some people searching for anything of value."

"I think I'll poke around all the same."

"Sure. But if you're going to search through all this, you'll need to take a bath and change clothes before we go out to dinner."

Bodie didn't hear him. The kid had picked up a piece of blackened iron and begun to poke through the deep bed of ashes.

"Homer, I hope you stay out of there," Longarm said. "With your thick coat you'd be impossible to clean up if you went in there with Bodie."

In answer, Homer trotted into the sea of ashes, and when he reached Bodie, he lay down with his head on his paws.

Longarm watched the pair for a few moments, then turned and headed back into town. His first stop would be the *Territorial Enterprise* newspaper office and he hoped to meet his old friend the reporter Dan DeQuille.

"No," the editor, whose name was Paul Elder, replied, "Dan has taken a short vacation and gone up to Lake Tahoe. I had to practically fire the man to get him to leave here for a few restful days. Dan really needed a break because being a newspaper reporter in a dying town isn't easy or pleasant work. Everyone up here is desperate, and all they talk about is when one of the few operating mines might make a big strike to get the money flowing again."

"Do you really expect that to happen?"

"No," Elder admitted, "I don't. This isn't the first mining town I've opened a newspaper in, and it probably won't be the last. But I'm still eking out a living and paying my bills, so I'll hang on until the very end . . . just like Dan. You know, I love this city, and I just can't stand to give up and abandon her to die."

"I admire your perseverance but question your good sense."

"I'm an old-time, died-in-the-wool newspaper editor, and instead of blood my veins flow with ink," the man said with a wry smile. "Nobody gets rich in this business, and you're always rocking the boat to keep up reader interest, so you make a lot of enemies. Did you know that the last editor down in Bodie wrote such an inflammatory article that the man who felt his name was tarnished charged into the newspaper office down there and shot the Bodie editor dead?"

"I wasn't aware of that."

"It happens all the time! If you only write good and happy stories and never criticize or point out corruption and injustice, pretty soon nobody wants to read your rag. But if you attack people and constantly stir the pot, people hang on your every word and some get mad enough to kill."

"Maybe you should write a book."

The editor, a tall, thin man in his early sixties, with gray muttonchop whiskers, laughed. "I *am* writing a book! One about wild Indians and brave cavalry soldiers and damsels in distress. And you know what?"

"What?"

"I'll bet my hack fiction sells a whole lot more copies than my newspaper."

They both laughed, and then Longarm said, "I'm here to investigate the Burlington murders and the torching of their mansion."

"Why?" Elder asked with his characteristic bluntness. "You're a *federal* marshal and this isn't a federal issue."

"It became one when United States Marshal Hugh Parker got involved and then was murdered for his trouble."

Elder raised a bony finger to the ceiling. "Oh, yes! Marshal Parker was found beaten to death behind a saloon down in Reno."

"That's right."

"And you think," the editor asked, "that the Burlington murders and the fatal beating of Marshal Parker are somehow . . . related?"

"I'm almost certain of it."

The editor of the *Territorial Enterprise* rubbed his pointy chin, and his eyes began to dance with excitement. "I'm feeling that maybe we've got a great story here! How about we go have a couple of beers and you tell me everything you know? I'll write a fine piece on it and it will stir the pot up to a boil."

"I'd rather you told me everything you know and

think might have happened regarding the deaths of Mr. and Mrs. Burlington and then I do some legwork. When the time comes, I'll be happy to tell you what I've found out and hopefully that I'm ready to make an arrest."

Paul Elder deflated a little but nodded. "All right. Let's go into my office where my typesetter can't overhear us. With Dan on vacation I'm the only writer, but I'm between stories . . . in fact, I'm pretty desperate to find any story."

"I'll give you one," Longarm promised, "and it'll come pretty soon. But now we need to talk in private."

Back in the editor's crowded office covered with old newspapers and odds and ends, they found two chairs and sat down across from each other.

"To begin with," the editor said, "we don't have any law enforcement up here. Our sheriff was laid off, and so when Marshal Parker arrived one day out of the blue to investigate the murders, everyone was surprised and happy. The Burlingtons, especially Chester, were much admired because they were generous in giving to the local charities."

"Go on."

"My first impression on the morning after the fire had died down enough to allow people to bring out the charred bodies was that it was an accidental death. Chester Burlington loved his cigars and his drinks. It happens all the time."

"But then the mortician found bullet holes in the skulls."

"Yes," Elder said. "And that changed everything.

The town went from mourning over the deaths of two of its most popular citizens into a state of anger and confusion."

"And suspicion?"

"That too," Elder admitted. "There were many in this dying town who thought that perhaps the couple had gotten drunk together and into a fight. One or the other killed their spouse, then—filled with sudden remorse—shot themselves."

"Squarely in the back of their own head?"

Elder shrugged his narrow shoulders. "The bullet holes were small-caliber. Possibly made by a little derringer." Elder reached behind his own head. "I could do it and so could either one of them."

"I suppose, but that just doesn't seem likely."

"No," the editor agreed, "it doesn't to me either. The most likely cause of death was that someone robbed the pair and shot them and torched their mansion to hide all evidence."

"And I understand that their safe was hanging open."

"Yes," Elder said. "And that supports the murder theory."

"All right," Longarm said, "let's assume that one of them did not shoot the other and then shoot themselves. That only leave us with a murderer."

"That's the way I see it and so did Marshal Parker. He wasn't an easy man to tolerate, that one, but he was smart and he was relentless in pursuit of the truth."

"I think he found it," Longarm said, "but before he could act on what he'd found, the true murderer or murderers got to him and tried to make his death appear to be just a common mugging that proved fatal."

"Yes, that is quite right."

"So do you have any suspicions as to who did kill the Burlingtons and then Marshal Hugh Parker?"

"Of course if have my suspicions. Who wouldn't?"

"And they are?"

"If I tell you, then you must not tell anyone else." Paul Elder wearily passed a hand across his eyes. "The one who had the most to gain . . . in fact, everything to gain, by the deaths of Chester and Ruby Burlington is Darnell Burlington."

Longarm leaned a little forward in his chair. "That would be Chester Burlington's only son?"

"Yes. Darnell is a dangerous, greedy, and devious young man. His father bought his love with a mine that once was quite valuable but is now about to be closed because it no longer produces enough ore to pay for its operating costs. Darnell has steadily watched his worth plummet, like most other mine and business owners here on the Comstock Lode."

"I understand he is also a gambler?"

"A very inept one. Darnell usually drinks too much and gambles foolishly."

"It sounds as if he is on the verge of becoming penniless."

"That's right. Penniless, reckless, and desperate."

"All motives for murder."

The editor nodded. "Within a few days of Marshal Hugh Parker's arrival, he had decided that Darnell was the prime suspect. He even confronted him in front in the Bucket of Blood Saloon one evening, and the two men got into a fistfight. I guess it was quite a battle, and when it ended, both men were bloody."

"But the marshal couldn't arrest Darnell without concrete proof that the man had murdered his own father and stepmother for his inheritance."

"That's right."

"Where can I find Darnell?"

"If he is in Virginia City, and he often leaves for weeks at a time to visit San Francisco's wild Barbary Coast, then you can usually find him at the Silver Dollar Saloon or the Bucket of Blood."

"I'll find him even if I have to go to San Francisco, and I'll find out what evidence Marshal Parker had finally gotten on Darnell."

"Do that and you'll do Virginia City a big favor. Darnell is as poison and deadly as a rattlesnake. He needs to be put behind bars."

"Or six feet under."

"Yes," Paul Elder agreed, "that too."

Longarm left the *Territorial Enterprise* ten minutes later. He didn't have a shred of evidence with which to arrest Darnell Burlington . . . but he knew that was his man, and one way or the other he was going to bring him to a gallows or shoot him stone dead.

Chapter 18

Out of the deep bed of ashes, Bodie had discovered a heavy silver platter and a foot-tall statue of a mounted warrior carved from a single piece of green stone. He'd spotted the rider's helmeted head just barely poking out of the ashes near one of the fireplaces, and Bodie's initial impression of it was that it represented some ancient, oriental fighter galloping into battle. When he'd spit on the statue and scrubbed it with the tattered cuff of his sleeve to remove a layer of grime, Bodie was surprised to see that both horse and rider were intricately carved.

Bodie decided that the statue was unlike anything he'd ever seen before and no doubt quite valuable. He set the horse and warrior beside the silver platter, then batted at his pants and shirt, which were coated with ash. There was a gusting wind and his face was masked by soot and his nostrils were plugged tight.

Bodie put a thumb to one nostril and blew hard. Black snot streaked from his nose, and then he noisily cleared his other clogged nostril.

"So," a tall man said, stepping out from behind a nearby building, "you found a silver plate and that jade statue. Nice work, boy."

Bodie's head jerked around in surprise. The man was fifty feet away and moving toward him when Homer began to growl. Bodie heard himself say, "Mister, this place belonged to my mother and her husband. I'm not stealin' anything."

The man paused, placed his hands on his hips, and laughed. "Of course you are!"

Bodie felt his mouth go dry and his heart pound. "I ain't! I just told you that this place belonged to my mother, whose name was Mrs. Ruby Burlington."

"I'll have to check on that, but you need to come with me."

"Where to?"

He considered the question for a moment. "Jail."

"You're a lawman?" Bodie asked, eyes looking for a badge.

"Yeah. That's right. I'm a federal marshal from San Francisco and you're nothing but a thief."

Bodie swallowed hard. His hand moved closer to the gun strapped just above his narrow hips. "Mister, I tell you I ain't stealin'!"

The rumble in Homer's throat was getting louder.

"Your wolf dog better not charge me or I'll shoot him dead."

Panicked by the threat of his dog being shot, Bodie glanced down at Homer. The hair of the massive dog's shoulders was standing straight up and his teeth were bared. "Mister, don't you . . ."

Bodie's voice froze as Homer attacked.

The lawman whipped out a gun and fired at Homer, striking him in the shoulder and knocking him sideways. Bodie went for his pistol as Homer somehow found it within himself to roll over twice, then regain his feet and lunge up from the ashes, going for the shooter's throat.

"No!" Bodie screamed as his hand clawed for his gun.

For a single terrifying split second, Bodie had no doubt that he was about to die. But then Homer was knocking the tall man onto his back and tearing at the lawman's throat. The man shrieked and thrashed under the weight of the huge animal and Bodie heard two muffled shots and Homer went still with his jaws clamped on the lawman's severed jugular vein.

The lawman was still alive and he fired again into the dog's body, so Bodie shot the gunman twice in the head without taking deliberate aim.

"Oh no!" Bodie howled, grabbing his dog and pulling him away from the lawman. He hugged Homer's massive head to his chest and began to rock back and forth on his knees. "Homer. Homer!"

Perhaps a minute or two had passed when Bodie heard shouts from the town below. He crawled to his feet, staring at the grisly sight of the lawman's ripped open throat and the two bullet holes still spouting blood from his forehead.

Bodie bitterly whispered, "This time they'll hang me for sure."

"Hey!"

Bodie jumped up and twisted around to see a knot of shouting men struggling up the steep hill toward him.

It was all that Bodie could do to tear himself away from his dog, but he had to run and run fast. He grabbed the jade horse and warrior and the silver platter, then took off racing over rocks and sage. Bodie decided that he would run until his lungs or legs gave out, whichever failed first. It was almost sundown, and if he could get away from those men, he'd find a way off the Comstock Lode in the dark.

Bodie still had a couple of bullets in his gun and more in his cartridge belt; he would use them dearly if it came to a choice between dying in a gun battle or swinging from a rope. He also had two treasures that had belonged to his mother, and he was sure he could sell them someplace for at least a hundred dollars.

"If I can get off this mountain and reach the Carson River and the cover of those cottonwoods, I'll have a chance," he gasped as he ran. "If I can get far enough, I sell Ma's treasures and reach the high Sierra Nevada Mountains where no one will ever find me."

His lungs were already on fire, and he kept dropping the silver platter, so he stopped and buried it in under some dirt and small rocks. He might live to come after it someday, and so he marked the spot and noted it well. The horse and oriental warrior were heavy, but he wasn't going to give them up for anything as the sun began to dip behind the nearby

Sierras. Bodie thought of the old mining town of Bodie. He still had a few friends there. His mother might have had hard times, but she'd helped people even worse off than herself and maybe they'd help him in turn. Help him escape a hangman's noose.

Maybe.

Darkness finally fell on the Comstock Lode, and still Bodie ran on and on, but much slower. In the faint moonlight, he was a thin, dark wraith, a laboring shadow and one truly cursed. His mother had always been cursed and her blood was his blood. Eyes fixed on the silver ribbon of the Carson River far below, Bodie began to weep because Homer was dead and now he was all on his own.

Chapter 19

Longarm stood over the bloody remains of a tall man that he had never seen before. "Is that Darnell Burlington?"

"No," a slack-jawed man whispered, face pale as he stared down at the horrific site, "his name was Charlie Singleton, but he worked at Darnell's mine. I think he was his foreman."

"That wolf dog just tore him apart before it got killed," another man choked out.

"I didn't like Charlie," a third mused, "but I'd not wish that kind of death on any man."

"Me neither."

Longarm studied the faces of the gathering crowd then looked off to the distance. The sun was almost down, and there wasn't going to be much of a moon tonight. Longarm knew that Bodie was out there running for his life, and he sure wished the kid had run to him for help instead.

"Anybody see what happened?"

They all shook their heads.

One man cleared his throat. "I heard screams and gunshots, but that's all. And I saw the kid take off running. The sun was low and in my eyes, but it looked to me like he was carrying something big and shiny."

Longarm knew that questioning anyone here was a waste of his time. "Where can I rent a good riding horse?" Longarm asked.

"Old Mike Meeker has a few he rents on the other end of town. He charges an arm and a leg, though."

"Anybody else?"

"Just Old Meeker."

One man edged up on the body and stared at it for a moment before exclaiming, "Charlie has two bullet holes in his face! That boy must have shot him to death. Don't know if Charlie was already dead because of the dog at his throat, but the kid put two slugs in Charlie's brain!"

"He and his ma were both bad blood. That kid will get hanged sooner or later."

Longarm turned to the men who were talking, and his words were clipped and hard. "Bodie was here looking for things that belonged to his family. He had a right to be here. Charlie Singleton obviously came upon the boy and started the trouble."

"That's not the way I see it," a big man with a potbelly and a dirty shirt growled.

Longarm was in a black mood, and he whirled

around and stepped toward the man. "It sounds like you were a friend of Charlie Singleton."

"One of his few," the fat man said, suddenly looking as if he wished he'd kept his mouth shut. "Charlie was hard, but he was always fair to me when I worked at the mine."

Longarm drove his hand forward, slamming the fat man in the chest and knocking him backward. "Yeah? Well he came here and he started trouble. He killed the boy's dog and maybe he even shot Bodie, who is out there someplace in the sagebrush maybe bleeding to death as we waste time here arguing about who did what."

"You don't have to be shovin' me around. I heard you was a federal lawman and brought that boy and his damned dog up here. You hadn't done that, Charlie would still be alive and—"

Longarm drove a thunderous left uppercut into the man's solar plexus. The fat man's mouth flew open like that of a fish tossed out of the water. He doubled over, and Longarm dropped him with a short but vicious right cross to the side of the jaw. The fat man struck the ground with his moon face, twitching and moaning.

"Jaysus, Marshal!" a businessman cried. "You didn't need to do that!"

"Yes, I did," Longarm growled, turning away from the crowd. At first light, he would rent a horse, toss a sack of supplies over the back of his saddle, and take up Bodie's trail. He was pretty sure it would lead toward the Carson River and then probably south along the slope of the Sierras, perhaps all the way down to the town of Bodie.

Longarm hated like hell to leave Virginia City. He wanted to confront Darnell Burlington, and when he did, it was not going to be friendly. But Bodie was on the run, and Longarm could not even imagine the state of that boy's mind after losing the only thing he had loved . . . Homer.

"If I don't find and save him," Longarm muttered as he stopped to buy a few supplies at the general store just before it was about to close, "he's going to do something that will either get him or someone else killed."

"So what happened up there?" the owner of the store asked. "I heard a rumor going around that that boy and his wolf dog killed somebody. You got a name for the dead man?"

"Charlie Singleton," Longarm said, grabbing a few supplies off shelves.

"The boy killed Charlie Singleton! Charlie was a tough and dangerous man."

"Not near tough enough," Longarm said, tossing his supplies on the counter. "How much I owe you?"

"Well hold on while I tally 'er up. You don't need to be snapping in my face, Marshal. Seems to me you brought someone up here that just killed a man."

"Give a figure, damn you!"

The owner jumped back and started to say something, but after taking a look into Longarm's eyes, he changed his mind and wrote a figure down, then handed it to Longarm.

Longarm paid the man and left in a hurry. He had bought a pint bottle of whiskey, a loaf of sourdough bread, cheese and some crackers, and a can of sardines. Mostly, though, when he thought of Bodie and Homer, he thirsted for the whiskey.

Chapter 20

Darnell Burlington despised horses, dirt, dust heat, or anything to do with the outdoors. But now, in a rented buggy with the last two of his trusted henchmen riding at his side, he was headed off the Comstock Lode. He was hot on the trail of a boy who, if he lived, could rob him of what should have been his very large inheritance.

Darnell was tired and irritable. When news had swept into town that Bodie had shot Charlie Singleton to death up by the burned-down Burlington mansion, Darnell was drunk and about to screw one of the town's most popular prostitutes, Sally Slide.

"We've got to go," Rafe Ward said, filling the doorway of Sally's hotel room.

"Get the hell out of here!" Darnell shouted.

"Boss, get your pants on and get your ass out of Sally's bed! Bodie gunned down Charlie and that kid is on the run. And you can bet that federal marshal will be taking up his trail in the morning. If we don't get to the kid before the marshal, it's all over."

"Shut up! I'll be along in a minute. Now close the damned door and get me a buggy."

Rafe gaped. "You want me to rent you a damned buggy?"

"That's right. You know I can't ride worth a shit."

"But we can't track . . ."

"Get moving!" Darnell bellowed, reaching for his pants.

"What's going on?" Sally Slide, also quite drunk, asked with a yawn as she squeezed her sweaty thighs together.

"Never you mind."

Sally's hand shot out, and she playfully cupped Darnell's balls. "What could be so important that you can't finish what you started, darlin'? I was just gettin' juicy."

"It's none of your business," Darnell hissed.

Sally's mood suddenly turned belligerent. "Well, dammit, Darnell, I expect to be paid even if you didn't finish."

Darnell slapped Sally Slide hard, splitting her lower lip and causing it to bleed.

"Damn you! I didn't do nothin' to deserve bein' hit in the face like that!"

"If you don't shut that big yap of yours," Darnell warned, "I'll slap your pretty face so hard it'll look like raw meat and nobody will want to screw you for the next month."

Sally Slide pulled a sheet over her exposed and still lovely body and dabbed at her bleeding lip with a dirty and stained corner. Her voice took on a whine. "Darnell, you never hit me before. You've cussed me out and did some hurtful things to my hole, but you never hit me in the face."

Darnell started to hit her again, but Sally Slide screamed so he tossed her a couple of dollars and headed for the door still half-undressed.

"You gonna kill that kid?" Sally yelled.

Darnell paused, one hand on the doorknob. "What did you say?"

Sally swallowed hard. "I said take care of yourself, Darnell. I forgive you for hittin' me just now, and I'll be waitin' when you return, and you won't have to pay for it."

"Smart girl," Darnell replied. "Real smart."

Darnell had left Virginia City within the hour, with Rafe Ward and Bull Halsey riding on either side of the buggy. They had passed through Gold Hill hearing the tinkling of piano music and the riotous laughter of drunken miners and saloon girls.

Darnell couldn't hold the buggy horse to a fast trot, and he was already getting tired whipping the old buckskin. "This gawdamn horse is so slow we'll be lucky to reach Carson City by dawn!"

"Sorry, Boss. These horses were all that Mike Meeker had to rent on such short notice."

"You can buy a better horse to pull that damned thing once we reach Carson City," Bull Halsey offered.

"How do we even know the kid is headed for Carson City?" Rafe Ward asked. "Maybe he struck out down this mountain headed for Reno."

"He doesn't know anyone in Reno," Darnell irritably explained, feeling hungover. "Did either of you dumb bastards think to bring a bottle?"

Their silence told Darnell that they had not.

"Well, when we reach Carson City, we'll buy something to drink."

"I still don't understand how we gonna find the kid," Rafe persisted.

"We'll wait and ambush him just south of town. I'm bettin' everything that the kid is headed for Bodie because he probably has a few friends there. All we have to do is be waiting."

"But if we don't find him then . . ."

"Then you and Bull will just keep ridin' until you *do* find him—and kill him." Darnell's mouth tasted like a shithouse and his stomach was giving him fits.

"How the hell did he manage to gun down Charlie?" Bull wanted to know.

"I have no idea," Darnell admitted. "But that ought to be a fair warning to us. When we find the kid, we move in close and shoot him down without any talk or hesitation."

"I never shot a kid before," Rafe said quietly. "Not sure that I want to start now."

Darnell laughed out loud and then hissed, "Rafe, you'll either shoot him or I'll pay Bull a hundred dollars to shoot the kid *and you*. How's that sound, Bull?"

The huge man riding an equally huge dun horse cackled. Rafe Ward tried to see if Bull and Darnell were serious, but it was too dark and he was pretty sure that they really *were* serious.

* * *

Just as Darnell, Rafe, and Bull were entering Carson City, less than twenty miles to the east, Longarm was striding into Mike Meeker's stable with a pair of saddlebags slung over his shoulder, a rifle in his left hand, and a sack of hurriedly gathered supplies in his right hand.

"I need a fast saddle horse in a hurry," he said, after pounding on Meeker's barn with the butt of his rifle.

"Gawdammit, I need my sleep!"

"A horse and make it quick," Longarm said, showing old man Meeker his federal officer's badge.

"I ain't got any rentals left right now."

"You have horses in that corral over yonder," Longarm said, pointing through the gloom.

"Them's my own two special horses. I don't rent 'em to anybody."

"You're renting the best of the pair to me right now," Longarm said. "Or selling. One way or the other, I'm taking a horse and I'm not going to jaw with you about it."

"Those horses are both real valuable."

"How much?"

"Fifty dollars."

"Sold—as long as the horse I choose comes with a bridle, bit, blanket, and saddle."

"Sixty dollars then."

"Fifty," Longarm insisted. "And you're robbing me blind."

Meeker was bent and ill-tempered. "What the hell is goin' on around here? Everybody wantin' to rent horses all of a sudden."

"Who are you talking about?"

"Darnell Burlington, Rafe Ward, and Bull Halsey all were actin' like their asses were afire last night, after that shootin', and wanted rental horses. What the hell is goin' on here? The Black Death or a fire or some damn thing about to hit this town at high noon?"

"Darnell Burlington rented a horse?"

"And a buggy. His two men rented saddle horses. They were all in a hurry. Were they after that kid that shot Charlie Singleton last evening?"

"You guessed it," Longarm admitted. "And if I don't find Bodie first, he's as good as dead."

"Ha!" Meeker exclaimed. "It's about a big damned inheritance, isn't it!"

"You're smarter than you look, old man. Now, help me get after those men before they find the kid and kill him."

Meeker tugged thoughtfully at his beard. "They burned down the mansion with Mr. Burlington and Mrs. Burlington in it, didn't they?"

"You missed your calling," Longarm said. "You should have been a Pinkerton detective."

"Sixty dollars and you're on your way, Marshal."

Longarm had just a little less than that left in his wallet. He pulled out all the bills and shoved them into the old man's outstretched hand. "This'll have to do."

Meeker counted the bills in the lamplight. "You're short a few dollars."

"Too bad. I'll have to send you the rest next time I get paid."

Meeker wasn't happy, but he nodded. "Are you a man of your word?"

"Yes, I am."

"Then take the sorrel gelding because he's the better animal," Meeker said. "I never liked Darnell, and those men are bad ones."

"Thanks for the warning." Longarm started off to halter the sorrel.

"Hope you save that boy," Meeker said, tagging along in his wake. "Ruby Burlington was a good woman. When she got lucky and married Chester Burlington, she didn't get uppity or put on any airs like you'd expect. If Darnell killed her and Chester, then I hope you kill him."

"That's my plan," Longarm said. "Now, if we could stop jawing, maybe I might even be able to save Ruby's boy."

Old Man Meeker scurried off, jamming the money into his back pocket.

Five minutes later, Longarm galloped out of Virginia City on a handsome sorrel with a blaze on its face, just as the sun was lifting off the sage-covered and broken-rock eastern mountains. In less than two hours, he was down on the flats, galloping parallel to the Carson River lined by its tall, water-loving cottonwoods. Longarm knew he was starting much too late to overtake Darnell and his gunmen. They'd be in Carson City by now, and maybe they'd already found and killed Bodie. Longarm had no way of knowing, so he just kept pushing the gelding to its limit without breaking its wind.

* * *

When he rode into Carson City at mid-morning, his horse was coated with sweat and lather even though the high desert early morning air was crisp and cool. He was looking for the buggy, horses and men Mike Meeker had told him about. He'd spot them if they were in town.

Longarm rode up and then back down the main street, where a few people were awake and moving to their jobs and daily businesses. He saw a couple of horses tied in from of the Gold Strike Saloon, but otherwise nothing.

"Where is the boy?" he kept whispering to himself. "Is Bodie hiding out in the sagebrush or maybe the cottonwoods down by the river? Or did he just bypass Carson City and keep walking? Maybe he's behind me and still up on Sun Mountain or on his way north to Reno."

There were so many questions that Longarm couldn't possibly answer. All he knew for sure was that this was a race against Darnell and his pair of hired killers. Bodie was already better than most with a six-gun, but he was no match for the three hunters close on his backtrail.

Chapter 21

"Have you seen a tall, dirty, and thin boy with long hair walking around town early this morning?" Longarm began to ask everyone he saw.

"There are a few of those kind around," one man replied. "I ain't seen any of 'em this morning, though."

"Thanks."

Longarm rode the sorrel over to a water tank and let it drink sparingly. He'd learned the hard way not to allow an overheated horse to drink too much cold water all at once. After a few minutes, he led the horse over to a hitching rail and tied it up and loosened its cinch. A few minutes later he walked over to the sheriff's office, which was closed. He was about to return to his horse and start circling the town looking for Bodie when the sheriff hailed him.

"Hey, mister, how can I help you this morning?"

Carson City's sheriff was a rugged-looking man probably in his early sixties. He had silver hair and a matching mustache and wore a friendly smile on his face.

"I'm a deputy United States marshal from Denver, looking for a runaway boy about fourteen or fifteen years old. He is tall, dirty, and unkempt, with a gun strapped on his hip, resting in a black leather holster."

"Sounds like you're looking for trouble."

"His name is Bodie. His mother and stepfather were murdered up on the Comstock Lode. Their last name was Burlington."

The lawman's smile evaporated. "You'd be talking about Chester Burlington and his new wife, Ruby, I reckon."

"That's right."

"What's the boy got to do with them?"

"He's Ruby's son. I believe the boy is due to inherit quite a lot of money, but I think Chester's son, Darnell, is trying to make sure that never happens."

"By doing what?"

"Murdering Bodie just like I think that he did the Burlington couple."

"Are you saying that Darnell shot his own father and then burned his body in that mansion fire?"

"That's exactly what I'm saying."

The sheriff shook his head. "I've met Darnell a few times, and once I even had to part his hair with the barrel of my pistol and toss him in jail for being so drunk and disorderly. He beat up on a whore and pulled a gun on a man he accused of cheating him at cards. Darnell is nothing like his father."

"So I've heard. Bodie was attacked last night by

one of Darnell's men. A fella named Charlie Singleton. Somehow, Bodie killed Singleton and probably
thought that he'd hang for it, so he went on the run."

"Him and that wolf dog of his?"

"Singleton shot the wolf dog but not before it tore
a hunk out of his throat, and then the kid finished
Singleton off with a couple of bullets through the
center of his forehead."

"That kid sounds pretty hard."

"He is that, but I also think that he's salvageable,"
Longarm replied. "But if I don't find him before Darnell and his hunters do, none of it matters, because
he'll be shot on sight."

"I don't envy you the job. Ruby came from the town
of Bodie. Is that where you're bound?"

"It is if I don't find the boy named Bodie hiding
out around here. He's on foot and maybe hurt."

"I'll keep my eyes peeled for him. You stayin'
around awhile?"

"Just long enough to rest my horse and make sure
that Bodie doesn't show up." Longarm hesitated.
"Sheriff, I'm dead broke. Any chance I could borrow
ten dollars from you until I get Denver to cough up
some more travel money?"

"I can do that."

"You have a telegraph office here?"

"Sure do."

"I'll wire for some money this morning before I
leave Carson City."

"Fair enough. And if you're still in town this evening, stay with me and my wife. Alice is a great cook
and we have a spare bedroom."

"Much obliged," Longarm said. "But if Bodie is lurking around here, I'll find him before then."

"What about Darnell and his boys?"

"If I run across them here in Carson City, I may call on your help."

The sheriff nodded. "I'll stand with you."

"I never doubted that for a moment," Longarm replied. "Now I'm going to get back on that sorrel and start riding around a little."

"If you need help . . . need anything, you just come runnin' and I'll do what I can. I'm not as quick with a gun as I used to be, but I'm still a damned good shot."

"Thanks, Sheriff."

Longarm returned to his horse, tightened the cinch, and mounted up. He rode the gelding back to the water trough, let it drink a few more long swallows, and then he reined it toward the river. If he were Bodie, that's where he'd be hiding right now.

Chapter 22

Longarm rode down near the Carson River, then followed it out a mile or two eastward, toward the little town of Dayton. He didn't see Bodie, yet he felt the boy must be nearby, unless he'd bought or stolen a horse. Bodie did have a few left of those gold nuggets he'd been given in Denver, and any one of them would have bought him a fast and saddled horse.

And then Longarm saw the kid moving at a crouch along the banks of the river. Longarm touched his heels to the sorrel, sending it forward at a gallop.

"Bodie!"

Bodie whirled at the sound of the voice, just as a rifle's shot rang out. The kid took off running fast along the riverbank as two mounted riders angled to cut off his escape. Longarm leaned forward in his saddle and drew his gun. He had never had much success shooting accurately from a running horse, and he didn't want to waste any bullets. But the horsemen were much closer to Bodie than he was, and they were about to overtake the kid and shoot him in the back.

Suddenly, Bodie veered hard up the riverbank, disappeared behind a fallen tree, and opened fire. Longarm did the same, and his surprise attack caught the two horsemen off guard. Flanked on both the front and the back, the hired gunmen were caught in deadly cross fire. They tried to make a run for it, but Bodie and Longarm emptied their pistols and knocked them out of their saddles. One man splashed into the river and the other was thrown off his mount and smashed into a dead tree. Their frightened horses stampeded through the cottonwoods and disappeared.

"Bodie!" Longarm shouted. "It's me, Marshal Long!"

The kid hadn't seen the federal marshal on a horse before, and he was so rattled that he almost turned his gun on Longarm.

"Bodie," Longarm said, drawing the sorrel to a stop at the edge of the river and dismounting. "Settle down, it's all right now."

But Bodie kept his gun up. "Marshal, I'm not going to hang for shooting that man in the head up in Virginia City. He killed Homer and he was going to shoot me next. So if that's—"

"I know that you killed Charlie Singleton in self-defense," Longarm answered. "Holster that pistol, kid. This fight is over."

Longarm threw an arm across the Bodie's shoulders. "I don't know which one of us shot those two, but I'm glad we got it settled in our favor."

"Who are they?" Bodie asked.

Before Longarm could answer, a rifle's shot boomed from a distance and the kid was knocked halfway around to collapse beside the Carson River. Longarm whirled and saw a man standing about a hundred yards downriver beside a buggy. The rifleman took careful aim and fired again, and this time Longarm felt the impact of a bullet slice deeply across his upper arm. He scooped Bodie up and charged deeper into the cottonwoods as more bullets tracked his desperate escape into hiding. Longarm's sorrel had already taken off, leaving him without a rifle.

Two more shots and Longarm had Bodie safely hidden behind cover. "How bad are you?"

"I dunno," the kid whispered. "I'm body shot and maybe I'll die."

Longarm tore off the kid's shirt and saw that the rifle's slug had entered just under a rib and exited through the kid's back. It was a bad wound and one that would bleed the boy out unless Longarm could get the hole plugged up in a real hurry.

He tore Bodie's shirt into patches and used them to bandage both the entry and exit holes. He then used his belt to bind the patches tightly to the kid's skinny body. "Bodie, I've got to get you into Carson City, to a doctor."

Bodie was still conscious. "First, you have to shoot that rifleman, Marshal. You try to take me out of here, he's gonna pick us both off."

"You're right."

"Kill him," Bodie hissed. "Kill him before he kills us!"

"I'm going after him, but I won't be long. Right now I'm going to reload both of our guns. If I don't make it back, Darnell will come to finish you off because he can't have any witnesses."

"Are you sure it's Darnell?"

"Yeah," Longarm said. "I only caught a glimpse of him, but it fit the description."

"Darnell murdered my ma and now he's almost killed me too."

"We'll get through this," Longarm vowed. "Just try to stay conscious in case he gets past me and comes to finish you off. You're the one standing between him and a lot of money."

"Money don't mean anything right now," Bodie said, teeth gritted in pain. "But I'll kill Darnell if he comes for me."

Longarm handed Bodie his reloaded pistol. "Stay down and don't move or make a sound unless you hear Darnell."

"Good luck, Marshal."

"Thanks, I'll need it."

Longarm left the kid and crawled deeper into the grove of cottonwoods. He peered around the trunk of a tree and saw the buggy clearly, as well as the two dead men.

But where was Darnell and his damned rifle!

Longarm had learned from hard experience that sometimes great patience was required even when patience was most difficult to summon. Darnell had a repeating rifle, so it was to his advantage to wait and make a long-range killing shot. Longarm had a bloody arm to prove that the gambler and mine owner was a fairly accurate shot.

"Wait for him to come for you," Longarm told himself. "Stay down and wait for him to get into the range of your pistol."

So Longarm waited, although he knew that Bodie was still losing a little of his precious blood with every passing minute. Finally, Longarm heard a sound and almost shot his horse, which had wandered back to the river and was drinking. Longarm watched the horse's ears, and when the sorrel raised its head suddenly and turned to stare, Longarm followed the animal's line of vision and caught a glimpse of Darnell slipping in closer.

"Wait until he comes to you," Longarm whispered softly to himself.

Agonizingly slow minutes passed. A pair of crows were squawking in the higher limbs of a nearby tree. Longarm glanced up at them and they seemed to be irritated by something down below.

Darnell.

Longarm took the actions of his sorrel horse and the pair of cawing crows to be good and important signs. Animals had sharper senses than he, and they were giving him a warning and directions toward his enemy.

"Closer. You got to come closer."

Ten minutes and the crows kept up their angry squawking until they flew away, and that's when Longarm knew that Darnell was right under their tree and possibly their nest.

Longarm stretched out on the ground, extended his gun in front of him, and laid it across a fallen limb. The gun was steady, and the air was hot and fetid with all the decaying wood and riverbank debris. Mosquitoes buzzed overhead and began to bite, and big flies, smelling fresh blood leaking from Longarm's upper arm, began to torment him even more.

But Longarm didn't move a muscle until Darnell finally stuck his head out to take a look. When the man didn't see a target, his upper body slowly emerged from cover, and that's when Longarm squeezed off a shot that punched Darnell squarely in the chest and sent him backpedaling and then crashing down into the deep, dead carpet of rotting leaves.

Longarm jumped up and ran forward firing, but it was wasted lead because Darnell had been shot through the heart.

The old buckskin hitched to the Meeker buggy wasn't able to run, but Longarm beat the animal into a trot while Bodie lay on the seat beside him hanging onto life by a thread.

"Where's the nearest doctor!" Longarm yelled as they entered Carson City.

"Just up the street!"

Longarm saw the doctor's sign, and the buckskin barely had time to come to a complete stop before Longarm jumped down, grabbed Bodie up into his arms, and rushed him inside.

"He's shot through the body, Doc! And he's lost a lot of blood."

"Bring him into my examining room!"

The next hour was one of the slowest that Longarm could ever remember. He paced back and forth in the waiting room like a caged animal, until the doctor emerged to say, "I think he's going to pull through this."

"Are you sure?" Longarm anxiously asked.

"Yes. The bullet passed through his body cleanly and didn't damage any organs. He's in shock from the loss of blood, but he's young and strong. Now I'd better take a look at that arm of yours," the doctor added. "You're not so young anymore."

"No," Longarm agreed, "but at least I'm still alive."

Epilogue

Almost five weeks later, Longarm and Bodie stepped down onto Denver's crowded railroad platform and met Billy Vail, along with Bodie's grandmother and aunt. While the two women hugged, fussed over, and even cried with happiness over the Kid from Bodie, Longarm and Billy stepped aside to have a private word.

"Custis, you look far more rested than you did when you left here with Bodie."

"I had a month to loaf around in Virginia City and Carson City waiting for a federal judge at the territorial capital to settle all the legal and financial issues relating to the Burlingtons' last will and testament. It was locked up in a bank vault, but Darnell Burlington had paid to have a very good forgery made giving him his estranged father's full inheritance. If John Stock hadn't arrived here with Bodie and that bloodstained letter we found, I'm pretty sure that Darnell

Burlington would have gotten away with a double murder and inherited his father's fortune."

"I see." Billy glanced over at Bodie and his doting relatives. "So I take it that the kid inherits *everything*?"

"Yes. We sold the mine for a song just to be rid of it. Maybe one day it will become productive again, but that's doubtful."

"So," Billy said, trying to understand, "if the mine was worthless and the family mansion located in Virginia City was nothing but a pile of ashes, what was left for him to inherit?"

"About forty-five thousand dollars and a real nice city lot in Reno that he's going to hang on to until its value goes up even more than now."

Billy Vail's eyes widened. "So Bodie is rich!"

"Yes, he is," Longarm agreed. "And all the way back from Reno on the train I talked to him about how to save and invest his money rather than squander it on foolish pleasures."

Billy burst into laughter. "Custis, you're the *last* person who could give anyone financial advice or warn him of expensive pleasures!"

Longarm grinned. "Well, that might be true, but I'm pretty sure that between his grandma Ida and aunt Rose, they'll keep a tight rein on Bodie."

"Is he going to live with those two doting women?"

"As long as he can stand it. Bodie is a smart kid, and he knows he needs to learn to read and write much better than he can now. He's also too old to go back to school and learn without the embarrassment of being surrounded by kids half his age. So I told him that his grandmother and aunt would almost certainly be willing to tutor him."

Billy glanced over at the fawning women. "I'll tell you this much: Bodie might be rich, but if I was him I'd rather strike out on my own than put up with those two overly protective women."

"My guess is that he just might do that."

"Where are you going?" Billy asked.

"I'm going to buy some flowers and visit Gloria's grave."

"But what about Bodie?"

"One thing I know for certain," Longarm called over his shoulder, "is Bodie can handle anything that comes his way all on his own."

And with that, Longarm grabbed up his bag and walked back into the city that he most loved.

GIANT-SIZED ADVENTURE FROM AVENGING ANGEL LONGARM.

BY TABOR EVANS

2006 Giant Edition:

LONGARM AND THE OUTLAW EMPRESS

2007 Giant Edition:

LONGARM AND THE GOLDEN EAGLE SHOOT-OUT

2008 Giant Edition:

LONGARM AND THE VALLEY OF SKULLS

2009 Giant Edition:

LONGARM AND THE LONE STAR TRACKDOWN

2010 Giant Edition:

LONGARM AND THE RAILROAD WAR

2013 Giant Edition:

LONGARM AND THE AMBUSH AT HOLY DEFIANCE

penguin.com/actionwesterns

M456AS0812

DON'T MISS A YEAR OF

Slocum Giant
by
Jake Logan

Slocum Giant 2004:
Slocum in the Secret
Service

Slocum Giant 2005:
Slocum and the Larcenous
Lady

Slocum Giant 2006:
Slocum and the Hanging
Horse

Slocum Giant 2007:
Slocum and the Celestial
Bones

Slocum Giant 2008:
Slocum and the Town
Killers

Slocum Giant 2009:
Slocum's Great
Race

Slocum Giant 2010:
Slocum Along
Rotten Row

Slocum Giant 2013:
Slocum and the Silver
City Harlot

penguin.com/actionwesterns

M457AS0812

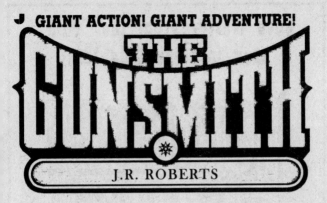

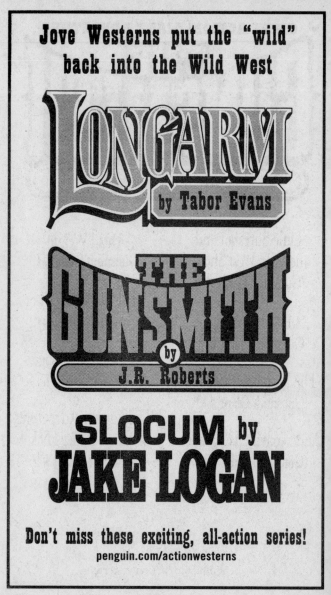